A Theocsbury Storyteller

M J David

Published by

MELROSE BOOKS

An Imprint of Melrose Press Limited
St Thomas Place, Ely
Cambridgeshire
CB7 4GG, UK
www.melrosebooks.co.uk

FIRST EDITION

Copyright © M J David 2017

The Author asserts his moral right to
be identified as the author of this work

Cover photo: **'Tewkesbury Abbey in Mist' courtesy of Jack Boskett Media LTD**

ISBN 978-1-912026-00-5
epub 978-1-912026-01-2
mobi 978-1-912026-02-9

All rights reserved. No part of this publication may be reproduced, stored in a retrieval system, or transmitted, in any form or by any means electronic, mechanical, photocopying, recording or otherwise, without the prior permission of the publishers.

This book is sold subject to the condition that it shall not, by way of trade or otherwise, be lent, re-sold, hired out or otherwise circulated without the publisher's prior consent in any form of binding or cover other than that in which it is published and without a similar condition including this condition being imposed on the subsequent purchaser.

Printed and bound in Great Britain by:
Airdrie Print Services Ltd
24-26 Flowerhill Street
Airdrie, North Lanarkshire
Scotland, ML6 6BH

This book is dedicated to the memory of my mother,
Georgina Joan Moss,
a lady who showed her family love.

Acknowledgements

Through the personal experiences in my life, I know I could never have achieved what I have in producing this collection of stories without the help, support and outright pushing from family and friends—and those who never actually realised they were doing me so much good.

I want to say thank you to my sister, Sue, and her husband, Nick. I will never be able to put into words anything that would, or could, ever repay you for what you did during the darkest time in my life and what you still do in keeping me grounded.

My two sons, Kevin and Richard. Between them they have shown me what it is, when there is unconditional love in a family. They make my heart swell with pride every day. They are the inspiration of a few of my stories and now that I am a granddad, I'm sure I will find inspiration for lots more. Christine and Maya, I see love reflected in you both and I can't wait to meet Ellie. I love you all with all my heart.

My partner, Pauline; you have been at my side for ever. You held out a hand when I tripped and fell—you helped me back on my feet. Saying thank you will never be enough. I just wish we had met earlier in life, to have enjoyed it—as we are—even more.

I would also like to say thanks to Pat Stevens, who had the unenviable task of reading the first two or three stories and then suggested I should pursue my writing.

Finally, thank you to Jill, Gwyn, Rachel, Michelle

and all the staff at Melrose Books; without your assistance, kind words, encouragement and patience, we would never have completed this project.

Contents

The Ultimate Answer Is …?	1
A Son's Journey Home	5
After Life	14
A Dream Knight for Sally	25
Visitors	38
Payback	43
A Second Time Around	52
Discovery	59
'Author … Author'	69
Verdict	76
Eternal	85
Secrets	94
A Father's Pain	98
Home for Christmas	108
Unanticipated	116
Demons	123
The Beautiful Game	128

The Ultimate Answer Is …?

Ruth was seated at the head of the long dining table, silently enjoying the hubbub of conversations going on around her. Holding her wine glass close to her lips with both hands, she was listening to the differing opinions of her guests to the question she had just posed as a subject for debate.

She watched as each of her guests made an individual argument and how the recipients engaged in some form of witty riposte to the statements being made, each student having agreed to recognise that there could only be six possible answers; the six being: who, where, why, what, when and how?

Ruth Blackman was Dean of Nevik University and held dinners each month for those students who showed potential in their chosen subjects. Reality was, she would eventually invite all students from the senior year to one of her famous dinners because she could not, and would not ever, single out anybody as being inferior of mind. She firmly believed that every student had good and not so good attributes to offer the new University.

Initially, the question she had posed had been met with complete and utter silence. She had studied each of her guests in turn, trying to see if there was any giveaway sign to their individual, personal answer. She watched as heads began to turn to others looking for some kind of inspiration or, indeed, an answer. The first to voice an opinion was a young man whom she knew to be studying law and English literature. He was quite adamant that the answer must surely be the question of when. This inspired another young man to counter with the question of where, which in turn had sparked a few raised voices for the more obvious how. The chatter amongst her guests was in full flow and she found herself smiling and nodding in agreement with anyone who garnered her favour, though offering no opinion as to a possible answer. For her, the object of the exercise was for them to find their own answer.

She noticed one student, a young lady, sitting at the far left of the long table, who appeared to be listening but not taking an active part in the debate. Ruth watched as the young lady listened intently to the argument put before her, but offered no alternative argument or response. Ruth found this fascinating since all the other students appeared to have more than one opinion, yet the young lady offered nothing of her own thoughts. Running a mental check, Ruth quickly came to the young lady's name, Joanne Pocket, studying English language and biochemistry. Ruth knew from recent reports and exam results that Joanne was doing exceptionally well, coming top of her class in both subjects. She watched the young lady as one after another of her fellow students tried to glean some form of response from her, but to no avail. Ruth became totally absorbed by this young woman's approach to the debate, listening and appearing to accept all and every statement made to her, but saying nothing. It was a first for Ruth. In all of her other dinner discussions, she had observed many arguments in the subjects she'd suggested; some had even become heated, but all had engaged every member at the dinner.

At the end of the meal, it was usual for the students

to 'retire' to the university library where discussions could continue, or they could leave and go to bed; very rarely did any student retire to bed. With stronger drinks in hand and the buzz of conversation still strong, Ruth deliberately positioned herself near to where Joanne was seated and again studied the young woman from a discreet distance. Her fascination for the young lady and her seemingly noncommittal outlook towards the objective, was captivating. Ruth noticed how the young lady reacted as each argument was laid before her. She saw how Joanne's eyes would flick from left to right as the thought registered and the final decision of where or how to log the information. Small hand gestures that mimicked the typing of letters and numbers on a keyboard helped her to analyse the data. Her left leg crossed over the right with the foot still, never waving or bobbing up and down. The young Joanne was in complete control of her senses and aware of her surroundings. Nothing seemed to be missed by the young lady.

Ruth checked the ornate clock sitting on the mantelpiece above the fireplace; it showed a quarter past one and she knew the debate must soon come to an end, as she herself had a busy day scheduled and most of the students had study periods to fulfil. She called the room to order and briefly sought the final thoughts of those gathered. The argument for each possible question was succinctly put by the cohort and she finally turned to Joanne for her insights.

Joanne slowly looked around the room, taking in the looks on the faces of her colleagues. She saw the eagerness in the eyes of each of them and smiled when her eyes came to rest on those of her mentor, Dr Ruth

Blackman. She gently placed her glass down on the small, round table to her side and coughed lightly to clear her throat. She remained seated when she spoke, her eyes slowly jumping from one fellow student to another.

"In the first instance, we know the proposed debate subject centres on our first thought and question, therefore we do not have to contemplate who, and there is no need to speculate. Having given our minds time to contemplate the subject question, I feel we would find our minds to be in considerable turmoil seeking the multitude of possible answers to the question of how. I believe we will consider, albeit briefly, when, because it has already been determined that we have been given time to consider. I further believe that through the question, we will ourselves have some kind of say with regard to where, again going back to the time element in the posed discussion subject. The 'what' will prove to be another multi-subject answer simply because, in itself, it poses more questions to the original subject. The initial examples I immediately think of are; what from, or even of what, etcetera, etcetera. So, in my conclusion of the debate, I find there is little doubt that we should consider the potential fact that the ultimate answer must be— a question. This negates the debate subject hypothesis since our first—our ultimate—thought or question must surely be … why?"

----- ~ -----

A Son's Journey Home

Jeff stepped up onto the Euroline coach and, although he knew in his heart he was doing the right thing, he was still nervous. He had been away for almost four years and the journey home was not going to be an easy one. With his backpack stowed, he settled in the seat at the back because he wanted to be left alone with his thoughts and tried to look uninterested as other travellers boarded. He checked his watch and glanced out at the fading light as the sun slowly slipped down over the distant mountains. He saw his reflection and vowed to shave his three-week-old beard when he reached the overnight stop, which was scheduled in six hours. He closed his eyes to the world around him, allowing him to replay the telephone conversation that had got him to where he was now, sitting on a coach waiting to leave Italy.

"Yes … I'm Jeffery Hunter … who is this and where did you get this number?" He remembered listening to the response and was surprised to learn that his older sister had given his location to the police in Gloucestershire. She was the only one in his family whom he'd been in contact with since he left, and he had made her promise never to give his family any information regarding his whereabouts—not even his mother, which had caused arguments between them. He had rationalised with her that if their mother knew where he was, and that he could be contacted by telephone, she would try to get in touch and talk him into going home and reconciling with his father.

His mind carried on with the telephone conversation, "Yes, I am the son of Mr Barry Hunter, why do you need to know?" He knew his tone of voice would give an impression of disinterest to that fact.

"Your mother and sister are very concerned about your father …"

"Really, Officer Delray, I'm not interested in anything about my father."

"I understand that Mr Hunter—may I call you Jeffery? We have been contacted by your sister, as a last resort so to speak, because it seems your father is …" —there was a long pause— "… well to be frank, your father is dying and your family wished to have you know what is happening. As you also know, your father was an officer with this force for many years and we are just passing on the information as requested and as a courtesy to your mother."

Jeffery felt surprisingly disturbed at the mention of his father being so ill and it had made him uncomfortable to feel like he did. He was also annoyed with his sister because of what she had done, since she knew the reasons why he'd left. He'd argued with himself for hours after the call trying to decide what would be the best thing to do. It was only after he'd really thought about the final piece of information from Officer Delray that he had made a decision. Officer Delray had said that his mother wasn't so well either and had pleaded for somebody to find Jeffery and tell him what was happening.

*

Jeffery woke with a start; the coach had obviously run over a pothole or something and had jolted him back.

He stretched out his legs as best he could and rubbed the stiffness from his neck whilst looking around the coach. Apart from the expected road noise, the coach was in virtual silence, although he could hear hushed whispers of conversation between fellow travellers. He pushed himself up against the seat and half stood so he could reach his backpack and, trying not to draw attention, he pulled on the strap. It swung down faster than he had anticipated and he wasn't quick enough to stop it from clipping the shoulder of the woman in the seat in front.

"Hey!" she exclaimed and turned in her seat. Jeffery apologised profusely and tried to sink down behind the backrest. "Thank you, young man … I was asleep," she said. Jeffery felt his whole body blush with embarrassment. "I … I … I'm so sorry … I didn't mean for it to fall on you … I am so terribly sorry." He half whispered, feeling all the eyes of the passengers turning and fixing on him. He quickly sat and slid down in his seat, hoping nobody would take any more notice, waiting for the excitement to die down before he moved again.

After about five minutes, he opened the pack and slipped out an old book he'd been reading and a bag of sandwiches he'd made for the journey. He thought he'd been able to do all of that with the minimum of noise, but he soon found out he was wrong. The woman from the seat in front stood, looked down at him, deftly stepped around the seats, and plonked herself down next to him. "Well …" she said, "if I can't sleep because you woke me, I think it only fair you talk with me to help make this ride a little more bearable. My name is Rachael, Mrs Rachael Sweeting." She pushed a hand forward, took his, and shook it quite vigorously. Jeffery blushed again. "Uh … hi … hello, I'm Jeffery, Jeffery Hunter … p … pleased to meet you Mrs Sweeting."

"Oh call me Rachael; after all, we will be travelling together for quite some time." She smiled.

*

By the time they had reached the overnight stop, Jeffery was surprised at himself for finding it so easy to talk with Mrs Sweeting—Rachael, a complete stranger. She was a homely type of woman and he was under her spell within an hour of their chatting. He was even more surprised when he'd told her of his relationship with his father and what had happened. He had fallen for her understanding heart and warm smile. She had listened to his story and offered little bits of insight and suggestions but had never offered or given him advice. She had let him talk and, in doing so, he had found solutions to what he thought were problems or situations and she gave a reassuring smile, which made him feel better for sharing. She reminded him of his mother, and when he had said so she rebuked him jokingly, suggesting she was not yet old enough to have such a young man as a son.

*

Jeffery had slept relatively well at the overnight stop hotel and was sufficiently refreshed when he boarded the coach at such an ungodly hour. He looked around for Mrs Sweeting but she didn't resume the journey. Her place in the seat in front was taken by an older gentleman who it seemed was intent on making everybody else's business his, and Jeffery sank down lower in the seat trying to avoid the glare of the man's eyes, but to no avail. He was pretending to read when the man spoke: "And ... where are you going young man? You should be working, not riding around on coaches at somebody else's expense." Jeffery remained still, giving the impression he was engrossed in the book he had in his hands, hoping the man would leave him alone, but the man reached through the gap between the headrests and flicked at the book. Jeffery looked up. "Oh, I'm sorry ... were you talking to me?" He glared back at the man. "Yes, yes, I was talking to you. I don't see any other young men sitting in the seats ... do you?" Jeffery looked along the seat then back at the man. "No sir I don't—actually, I'm rather busy—if you don't mind." He knew his response was terse but he really didn't want to spend any time with the man and returned back to his book. He was amazed when the man reached forward, taking the book and flipping it round to look at the title. "You won't learn anything from this drivel ..." He tossed the book into the space at Jeffery's side. "You need to be reading something that will expand your mind ... something that will help you understand the world, how it works and the part you have to play in it. Reading silly, stupid fantasy action fiction won't help you in any shape or form." They held each other's gaze for a moment, Jeffery started to think of his father and how this man—this stranger— sounded so much like the man he had walked away from all those years ago. "Yes, sir, and obviously you know better." He picked up the book and flipped the pages to where he had been reading. "And a very fine man he probably is," the old gent replied. Jeffery tried his best to ignore the man and realised he'd be stuck with him for the next part of the journey, silently wishing he'd left sufficient funds in his savings so that he could've taken a flight back.

Over the next few hours, Jeffery listened to the man and how he thought the world had 'gone to pot' since the majority of nations had abolished national service, how the young of today didn't really appreciate what they owed his generation. Whenever he tried to give his views, he was instantly put down and told that he had very little to offer the world since he had obviously decided to walk away from any and all responsibility. In truth, most of the time he'd spent with the man, Jeffery sat there wishing he were elsewhere.

*

By lunchtime, the coach had reached its next scheduled stop, Jeffery was glad to get off to stretch his legs and get away from the man, but he wasn't so lucky. After he had freshened up and purchased a sandwich and coffee, he was more than dismayed to see the man heading straight for his table. He turned away in the hope that the man would get the subtle message, but he failed. "I hope this chair is vacant, young man …" Jeffery turned back and said, "Actually sir," he started, "I would prefer you not to sit at this table—I would like some time to myself. I have a lot of things on my mind and I really don't think listening to you any longer will do me any good." He paused, looking directly into the man's eyes, willing him to walk away. The man hesitated for a moment then pulled the chair and sat down. "I think, young man, you need to learn a few manners … I have given you the best of my thoughts and you seem to have decided to ignore everything I've said and advised. It would be remiss of me to allow that to happen—especially as you say you have many things on your mind. Two heads as they say …" Jeffery interrupted him. "Sir, I have listened to everything you have said and, to be fair, some of it I agree with and some I do not. However, I would appreciate it if you would leave me alone and allow whatever is to be—to be." He picked up his coffee and sandwich then leaned forward and, half whispering, said, "Sir, you sound just like my father and I didn't agree with most of what he said either, but he is very ill in hospital and I am travelling back to England so that I can be with him and my family." He held the man's gaze for a moment longer then turned and walked away.

Jeffery had settled himself in his seat on the coach, expecting the man to reappear at any moment. He was feeling guilty after speaking to him so harshly and wanted to apologise, but the man never returned. When the coach pulled away, he felt all the more uncomfortable. After a while, he stopped thinking about the man and closed his eyes; he was on the final leg of the journey before they boarded the ferry and he needed time to think—he still didn't know what he was going to say to his father … a man he had left out of his life for so long.

*

At the ferry port, he had called his sister to let her know where he was and what time he expected to arrive in England. She had given him an update on their father and promised to be at arrivals to collect him when they docked.

He emerged from customs looking around, hitching his pack onto his shoulder, he saw his sister. She was standing next to a tall police officer; they waved when they saw him and he quickly walked over to them. His sister Sandra explained, as they walked out into the cold night, the drizzle of light rain forcing them to huddle under the umbrella she was carrying, the officer out in front of them.

In the car, as they sped towards Gloucestershire, Jeffery listened to everything Sandra said, his mind doing cartwheels at the potential prospects he was now facing. She told him how their father was in dire need of a kidney and that the hospital had not found any suitable donors, but they thought, hoped, Jeffery would be—if he was willing. He turned to look out of the window, streaks of rain rolling across the pane and he thought how things had changed so dramatically for him in the last forty-something hours. His conversation with Mrs Sweeting and that obnoxious man filtered through as he wondered what he should do.

"Every father is hardest on his first son …" Mrs Sweeting's voice filled his head, "… it is primal, a need to make sure that every part of him continues—his genes continued and that includes the very basic of characteristics." Jeffery smiled at the thought of Mrs Sweeting and the way she had allowed him to talk and figure things out for himself. He wondered where she was now. Then he thought about the man, remembering how he had treated him; instantly refuelling his guilt. He recalled the pained look on the man's face as he had walked away from the café table and the terrible words he'd whispered at him. He turned back to his sister, "So, what you're saying is that I—could be a match for him … for Dad." Sandra half smiled, "Yep, 'fraid so brother but …"

"But what? You say he needs a transplant and that I'm most likely to be a match."

Sandra took his hand. "Nobody will be expecting you to do it, Jeff, especially how things have been between you all these years." Jeffery frowned; he had never liked being called by his shortened name and then remembered how his father had insisted; all through his childhood he'd keep reminding people that his name was Jeffery, not Jeff, or any other shorter version. He allowed his mind to wander back and a lump formed in his throat as he recalled more memories of the things his father had taught him over the years—and the ones he recognised in himself. Times they had spent together began to flow freely, how they had built planter boxes for growing flowers and veggies. He absent-mindedly rubbed his chin when he remembered how his father had shown him how to shave properly. He turned to Sandra. "We—I need to get there quicker, sis, Dad needs me and I'll do whatever it takes to help him." Sandra looked at him wiping away the tears from his face. "I knew you would, Jeffery … you're just like him."

*

Three months had passed and Jeffery was sitting in a recliner in the conservatory reading. "Oh, I suppose you think that since you donated your kidney to me, you get to sit in my favourite chair." Jeffery looked up to see his father standing in the doorway smiling at him. "Morning Dad—actually I was waiting for you, I wanted to ask if you feel up to finishing off those planters we started at the weekend."

----- ~ -----

After Life

"Well, that's what I believe, Charlotte," Tracey said as she walked back to her desk with two cups of coffee in her hands. Charlotte watched in silence. They had had similar conversations about the subject over the past few months and now it was getting tedious; she would have to say something that would stop the whole thing from rearing its head again. She reached over and took one of the cups and placed it next to her computer, turning the handle towards herself. "OK, OK. We will have to agree to disagree then," she said. Tracey seemed not to hear and continued, "You see a bright light … then whoosh—you're gone." Charlotte sighed heavily. "OK Tracey, I get it; you don't believe in life after death, but I'm not so sure … OK?" Tracey looked over to her friend and smiled. "Look, I might be wrong, it could be that there is something—some other … existence or whatever, we will never know for certain—or at least until it's our turn." She picked up her coffee and took a sip. "Wow, that's really hot … be careful when you drink yours." Charlotte continued to watch Tracey as she set about going back to her work. She remembered how good to her she had been when she needed someone after her mother had passed away. She picked up her coffee and blew softly over the rim across the hot liquid before taking a sip, her mind back to happy memories of her mother.

For more than three years, Charlotte had fixated on what happens after somebody dies. She missed her mother terribly and had started doing research soon after her mother had passed and bought, found and borrowed all sorts of information on the subject. She had spent hundreds if not thousands of hours reading and even attending seminars on the subject. Her obsession had taken its toll on her relationships and a few friendships ... with the exception of Tracey at work. There were whispers around the office but she had eventually learned to ignore them, putting it down to their ignorance and fear of the subject. She knew that her neighbours whispered about her around the cul-de-sac; some thought she was a witch or high priestess of some sort of black magic coven. She'd got used to being shunned and sometimes thought it was a blessing in disguise because it meant she was left alone. However, it was something she was interested in and she was determined to find an answer—if there was one.

*

When Charlotte parked her car on the driveway to her house, she was still thinking random thoughts about her mother; it had become a habit and one she was reluctant to give up. As she approached the front door, she glanced around, since it was another habit, to take in the neighbourhood, to see if anything had changed during her day at work and, as usual, nothing had. It still made her smile whenever she thought about what her neighbours thought of her; a single, mid-thirty-something woman living in the big old house where her mother had passed away. She had moved in almost immediately after the funeral and had redecorated the whole place from top to bottom—literally. She knew that if any of them had actually taken an interest they would have found how different and bright it was in the house now. It had taken quite a few months of long evenings and late nights as well as busy weekends but she was happy and comfortable with the end result.

In the hallway, she dropped her bag next to the ornate hat stand and picked up the mail, placing it neatly on the hall table where she fussed with a loose flower head that had dropped. She removed her coat, hung it on the stand, then picked up the mail and went to the kitchen. When she walked into the room she immediately knew things weren't right—things were not as she had left them that morning. There was a hint of a smell—gas. She looked at the cooker hob and one of the rings was on. Then she noticed the cutlery drawer was open and the drainer wasn't folded away. A shiver ran down her spine; she always left the house tidy before going off to work. She went over and checked the back door, pulling gently down on the handle making sure it was still locked—it was. She checked the window, and that was also locked. She looked around the room, seeing if anything else was amiss and when she had satisfied herself that everything was as it should be, she turned the gas ring off and pushed the drawer closed. She put the mail down on the table that was placed central to the room, then folded away the drainer and put it where it should have been, next to the kettle, to the left of the sink.

After a moment's thought, she flipped the switch of the kettle and set about making herself a cup of herbal tea. She pulled a chair from under the table and sat down to go through her mail; another habit she had adopted since moving into the house. One of the packages caught her eye and she eagerly opened it. It was a paperback book she'd read about in a magazine and had sent away for some months ago but forgotten she'd ordered. She flipped its pages, catching a few words and phrases as each page flicked past. When she reached the end cover she placed it face down on the table and decided to read it later, after she'd showered and eaten.

*

After her meal and quick shower, she settled in the lounge, next to the hearth, her dressing gown wrapped tightly around her, tied securely at the waist. On the small occasional table next to her favourite comfortable chair was a small glass of Bushmills Irish Whiskey, a twelve-year-old single malt; an indulgence she'd taken to after she discovered a number of boxes hidden at the back of her mother's wardrobe in the back bedroom. She picked up her new book, carefully opened the front cover and began to read.

She was halfway through the third chapter when she heard what she thought was a cough coming from upstairs somewhere, but dismissed it as a result of the wind that had picked up over the last hour or so and went back to her reading. She was interrupted again by what she was convinced was somebody going through the cupboards or the chest of drawers in her bedroom. She put the book down on the side table, open at the page she had just finished, and slipped off the chair and went to the lounge doorway, stopping to listen for a moment. After a while she realised that she was holding her breath and slowly exhaled, not wanting to make a sound and in case she missed the noise again. Then, pulling the door open slowly, she quickly glanced back to the hearth and considered taking the fire poker—just in case but decided not to bother as it was probably the wind or something.

She didn't hear anything and turned to go back to the lounge and back to her book when there was a loud crash that came from her bedroom. She didn't hesitate, she rushed up the stairs, taking them two at a time, and when she got to her bedroom door she paused, listening for movement or any indication of somebody being in her room, her house—un-invited. She heard nothing and pushed the door open. In the dim light she could see very little so reached up and flicked on the light switch. The room, as far as she could tell, was undisturbed; everything was as she had left it after her shower; the towel was folded neatly on the ottoman at the end of her bed, her work clothes were still in a heap on the chair and her wardrobe still had its doors closed. As she stepped over the threshold of the room, she felt her heart pounding but she felt calm. There was an inviting warmth in the room and a sweet fragrance—of roses, she thought to herself. The hairs on her arms stood on end and her face began to tingle—as though somebody was gently brushing a hand over her cheeks and down her neck. She felt a comfort she had not felt in a long time—at least not since her mother passed. She smiled at what she was experiencing—was her mother's spirit visiting?

Suddenly there was a loud crash from downstairs, as though somebody had slammed the cutlery drawer shut. She almost flew down the stairs and into the kitchen; the lights were on, although she was positive she'd switched them off earlier. She looked around but nothing seemed to be out of place; she checked the back door and the window, but both were secure. She opened the cutlery drawer and everything was 'as normal', just as she had left it. A shiver spiralled down her spine but she didn't feel afraid; in fact, she felt more at home than she had in a long time. With a final check of the room, she switched the light off and went back to the lounge. When she entered she saw that her book was now closed and straight on the side table and her glass of whiskey was empty.

She paused, motionless in the room then spoke, "Is that you mum? Are you here with me?" Immediately, she felt silly for talking to the emptiness of the room—talking to herself. This sparked a few more questions that she asked out loud. "You know that's the first sign of madness ... talking to yourself." She answered herself, "Yep ... I know but I also know that ninety-eight per cent of people in this world talk to themselves, so I'm in good company." She smiled and checked the time on the clock sitting on the mantelpiece which showed it was almost midnight and she decided it was time to go to bed.

*

The minute hand of the alarm clock clicked over to half-past two, it was dark and Charlotte stirred when she became aware that her hand was being touched—lifted into the air. She opened her eyes, afraid she might see something she didn't want to and give away, to whomever was there, that she was now awake. Immediately she could see what she was certain was the form of a body leaning over her. The shape moved away and Charlotte could make out the outline of what appeared to be the silhouette of a body … a human form that was hazy against the darkness of the room. There was no detail in the form so she couldn't say for sure if it was indeed human. She sat up and stared. Her initial fear subsided and was replaced by the same warmth of calm she had experienced earlier. As her eyes adjusted to the darkness, she could see that her room seemed darker than usual and the form, although dark in its appearance, was not equal to the room. She watched as it moved to the end of the bed then stopped and lowered down, as though to sit on the ottoman. She leaned over and switched on the bedside lamp but its light did not penetrate the darkness. She looked at it, wondering if the bulb had blown and saw that it had created an umbrella-like thinning within the darkness, forming a greyness against the black. She looked back at the silhouette then over to the window; she could just make out the outline of the frame of the window and what she thought was the net curtains gently wafting in a light breeze.

Her gaze went back to the silhouette and she tried to speak but the words in her head wouldn't come through. She felt she was being drawn into the darkness, the skin on her exposed arms feeling just as her face had earlier when she had heard the noise, but she felt a peacefulness, a calmness wrapping itself around her. She heard what she thought was a question but was sure it hadn't been spoken; it felt as though she had actually felt the words rather than heard them. She tried to answer but again, the words in her head wouldn't form as speech. And again she felt the voice from inside her, "What is it you seek?" She again tried to answer and again the words wouldn't come out. She could feel her frustration rising. "What is it you seek?" The question was repeated. She thought for a moment, then concentrated on giving her answer through her mind and suddenly she felt her own voice, "Who are you?" She waited but felt nothing. She tried again: "Who are you?"

The silhouette moved to the side of her bed towards the window and she thought it was about to leave. She thought, "Please, don't go. Who are you? Why are you here?" The silhouette stopped moving and she felt the same sensation as before. "What is it you seek?" Her arms began to tingle and she looked down at her hands and saw that her fingers had begun to merge with the darkness and she immediately pulled her hands back to her chest. She looked at the silhouette. "Who are you?" she thought.

Suddenly the curtains at the window billowed upwards but there was no wind. She closed her eyes and concentrated. "Who are you?" she asked. The silhouette seemed to float to the other side of the room and settled on her chair. She could hear herself breathing and tried to control it. "What is it you seek?" The question sounded as though it was asked in frustration. She closed her eyes, concentrating. "What happens … to us … after we stop breathing—when we die?" Suddenly the room went deathly cold and she felt an icy breeze whip around her face and shoulders. She tensed as her fear started to rise but it was soon dissipated by a deeper feeling of warmth. She opened her eyes. "I want … need to know… what happens to us when we die? I want to know if there is a life after death?" Tears formed and she bowed her head and quickly wiped them away and looked up at the silhouette. "I want to know if my mother is there, is she happy? Can she tell me … can you tell me?"

Her voice was clear and she wondered if she was going crazy, talking to thin air. The silence grew louder as she struggled to hear. The silhouette remained still and Charlotte wondered if all this was in fact a dream. She shifted in her bed pulling her legs up to her chest, just like she did when she was a child and rested her chin on her knees, spellbound by the mysterious entity. She felt tired and tried to focus on the motionless form in the corner of her bedroom, but her eyelids slowly closed; she felt calm and almost unconscious. She thought she saw differences in the density of darkness, as though more silhouettes had entered the room and she found herself staring as each one floated around. Then it all went black and the voice inside her came back: "Why do you ask this?" At first she couldn't find the answer—she couldn't 'think' of what to say but then it came to her. "There are many theories about death and the 'hereafter'; I have read so many books and researched for so long—I ask because I am curious." As she 'thought' her reply, images filled her mind, the books and magazines she'd read, things she'd seen on television and heard on talk shows but, as they faded away, and her thoughts repeated themselves over and over she thought another response: "I ask because— because I am afraid." She shivered as her thoughts sent out her words, and the more she thought the clearer her fear manifested itself inside her entire body until it finally registered in her head; she was afraid of death—of dying.

The revelation of her statement woke her and her fear grew. She gazed about the room thinking she had dreamt the whole thing until, in the corner of her eye, she saw the silhouette. She immediately sat up, her heart pounding, her thoughts racing from one different fear about death to another. She began to tremble but was soon wrapped in the warmth she had experienced before. "What is it you fear of death?" the voice inside her head asked. She felt confused because the voice was soft and welcoming, as if inviting her into the darkness. She shook her head, trying to clear her thoughts—to stop thinking of death and dying. "There is nothing to fear in death," the voice continued.

Her mind began to race through old memories and she could see images of when she was very young; her mother and her at the seaside, the faintest of images of a man—probably her father. Then she saw the time when she had gone to the hospital with her mother and the doctor telling them the outcome of the biopsy and showing them an X-ray. Her whole body shivered at that memory. Finally, she could see herself at her mother's funeral; she saw the trees blossoming and the sun in the sky. She could feel its rays on her face and the warmth from the gentle breeze; another shiver ran down her spine. Suddenly, a feeling of complete loneliness filled her, as though she had been left behind on some important occasion. Tears burned at the corners of her eyes and she thought of her mother; questions filtered through her mind until her tears flowed uninterrupted.

She reached over in the darkness for a tissue and felt what she thought was a hand taking hers. She wiped her eyes with the back of her free hand and tried to focus. She saw that the silhouette had moved and was now at her bedside, her hand inside the form. Her instinct was to pull it free but a calmness filled her and she allowed her hand to remain. The voice came back, "There is nothing to fear in death, Charlotte my love." Charlotte tensed when she felt her name being spoken and immediately thought, 'Who are you? How do you know me—my name?' The voice repeated, "There is nothing to fear in death Charlotte, it can be shown to you." There was a pause and suddenly Charlotte became aware of her surroundings, of where she was, and what was happening. She recognised the furniture in her bedroom, the bedside tables, the curtains up at the window and remembered that she'd already picked out new material so she could make new ones—curtains that would reach down to the floor. Then she remembered how she had made plans for the summer and the colours she was going to use when redecorating the lounge and hallway. There were so many things she still wanted—needed to do. "Do you wish to see Charlotte?" the voice came back. A pained smile formed on her lips and more tears filled her eyes— "I—I—I don't know," she said softly.

----- ~ -----

A Dream Knight for Sally

"Oh come on Sally … you're still living your life in a dream world," Marion scorned.

Sally looked at her friend, then turned away and got up from the kitchen table, picking up the coffee cups. "Not all the time Mari—not all the time. Everybody should have *'their'* 'happily ever after' to look forward to," she almost whispered and went to the sink, placed the two cups into the bowl and turned on the tap to let the cups soak.

Sally and Marion had been friends almost all their lives. They had gone to the same schools, from infants through to seniors—and beyond. They had shared birthday parties, school dances and summer holidays together and at times were so inseparable that those that didn't know them thought they were sisters. There was even a time when, in their early teen years and after discovering 'boys', they had even dated the same boy—although not at the same time. As they grew older it was Sally who had wanted what she always thought of as normal; a loving husband, two or three children, a career and a nice home where they would all live happily ever after. Marion had focused more on her career, and only after lengthy and sometimes heated debates, agreed to go on a blind date with Sally and Gerry, if only to 'shut them up' about her life not being complete.

Since her divorce, Sally had grown to accept a life without a loving husband or children; she had a lovely home of her own and a stimulating career which was giving her all she thought she wanted from life. To her family and friends, Sally Church was the kind of person you could rely upon; someone who would be there if and when you needed her. She was seen as a strong independent woman without a care in the world and it was only her best friend Marion who knew different. Marion knew that in private, Sally Church was a lonely woman. Matters weren't helped either when Marion reminded her friend that she had a tendency to see life through rose-tinted glasses—always expecting the 'happily ever after' to become a reality. Marion had seen the change in her friend's demeanour when she had discovered she couldn't have children. For as long as she could remember, Marion knew that Sally had always wanted to be a mother, as Gerry wanted to be a father; however, their lives together were not to be blessed with such miracles and it was more than likely that this sad fact was the catalyst that finally drove Gerry away and the only reason why they eventually went their separate ways.

Standing at the sink, Sally took in a deep breath and slowly exhaled; she knew in her heart what Marion was trying to do, but was reluctant to take that final step. She turned and smiled. "I know what you're saying Mari and I do appreciate it, really I do, but …" she hesitated, "I'm just not ready—you know, not just yet, I need a little more time that's all."

Marion frowned. "Sally Church, you are the last person on this earth whom I would suspect of being afraid …" —her tone was less scornful— "and that's all it is, fear."

Sally smiled and went to her friend, placing her hand on her shoulder. "I know … I know."

Marion reached up and gently squeezed Sally's hand. "Who was it that told me only five, six years ago that fear is an acronym for 'false evidence appearing real'?"

Sally's smile grew wider. "Why that would've been me of course; when you were trying to back out of that blind date I'd—we'd set you up for." Sally and her ex-husband, Gerry, had cajoled Marion into going with them on a dinner date, where they had persuaded a friend of Gerry's to go too, because he was in a similar situation to Marion. That was nearly three years ago and they were now happily married and had been for two years or more.

*

A few weeks later, Marion was at Sally's for one of their monthly 'natter nights' as they called them; an evening where they would share a pizza and catch up with each other; they would share the latest gossip or sometimes try to put the world to rights or—just simply spend the evening together. They were relaxed, sitting opposite each other on the large comfy sofa, cushions wedged behind and to their sides. They had chatted about every subject under the sun when Marion leaned forward. "OK … what is it you're not telling me, Sally Church? You've had a silly smirk on your face ever since I got here … now spill." She held her friend's gaze for a while then leaned back, shuffling her midriff to make herself comfortable in the deep cushion.

Sally felt her face begin to redden and turned away. "Oh no … oh no!"

Marion leaned forward again. "I know you far too well, Sal, and I know you're hiding something, so don't try kidding the kidder. Take a deep breath and tell me that secret you've been dying to tell me all evening."

The sharpness of her tone took Sally by surprise, but when she saw the warmth of the smile she mellowed, and although her cheeks were almost crimson, she put her glass down on the table next to the sofa and turned to her friend. Then, in an almost teenage giggle, blurted out her news: "I've met someone, Mari. I've met someone."

The shrieks that followed would have woken the dead. Marion nearly dropped her glass as she tried to place it down and give her friend a hug—all at the same time. Sally had lurched forward nearly knocking her own glass over when her legs swung out as she too tried to hug her best friend. They hugged each other, bouncing up and down, their giggles and cries seemed to last for ages as each tried to say something to the other, but neither hearing what was being said.

As their excitement died, Marion reached over and took Sally's hand in hers. "I am so pleased for you, Sal, so pleased, now ..." she paused, reached back for the fallen cushions on her side of the sofa and slipped them back into place, picked up her wine and leaned back, "... now tell me everything ... and I mean every-thing." She almost spelled out the last part of the word, "I want details—times, places, height, weight, eye colour, where he works, how much he earns ... the lot." She took a sip of her wine then rested the glass in her lap, waiting for the response.

When Sally had caught her breath, she too took a sip of wine and no matter how hard she tried, she just couldn't stop smiling. "W-e-l-l ..." she began, "he works in finance, he's tall-ish, about five eleven maybe six foot, he has drop-dead gorgeous blue eyes, a hint of grey in his hair and he's sophisticated, intelligent, well-spoken and … oh so much more …" she finished with a sigh.

Marion watched, wide-eyed as her friend spoke dreamily of the man she had met. "What's his name? What's his name?" she asked eagerly.

Sally stared for a moment and looked at her wine glass. "Uh … I don't know … yet."

Marion nearly choked on her wine. "WHAT!" she exclaimed. "You don't know his name …" she paused, watching Sally wriggle uncomfortably in her seat. "Sally Church …" she scorned. Sally continued to look away. "Oh no, Sal … plee-ase don't tell me he's a figment of your imagination; someone you've only 'see-een' walking in one of those endless corridors at your works … plee-ase, Sal, don't say that." The whine in her voice trailed off. "Is he actually real, Sal?" she asked sternly.

Sally snapped around to face her friend, "Of course he's real, Mari … I'm not in the habit of making things up … am I?"

After a moment's silence between them, Mari leaned over and took Sally's hand. "I'm sorry, Sal, I didn't mean to bite."

Sally smiled. "That's OK, I know you didn't and I understand why you might think that anyway." After another moment's silence, Sally shifted in her seat and smiled broadly. "Well …" she said with renewed excitement, "I think he's noticed me too. He was in our department the other morning and I could feel his eyes on me—you know? That feeling you get when the hairs on the back of your neck stand up and it sends shivers down your spine."

Mari smiled back. "Oh I know that feeling." The rest of the evening passed as usual and they laughed at the predicament Sally had got herself into; their friendship secure as ever. When it was time for Marion to go, she turned at the doorstep and said, "Are we still on for Saturday morning?"

Sally gave her a hug and whispered, "Of course we are, I always look forward to our Saturdays at the market and shopping … our girls' day out."

*

Steve Appleton was sitting at his desk in the study when his son Alex walked in. He slowly walked over to where his father was working and waited. Steve glanced at his son quickly then back to the screen of the laptop.

"All your homework done then?" he asked.

Alex nodded and leaned on the desk's edge. "Da-ad … can we go to the market on Saturday morning."

Steve finished tapping the keys and swung his chair around so he could face Alex. "I don't see why not. What are you hoping to get this time?" Alex looked down to the floor, but said nothing.

Steve pulled Alex towards him. "Come on, Alex, I know you don't want to go to the market just to look around, what do you want to get?" Alex lifted his head and stared into space for a moment, then focused on his father. "I want to buy a new fishing reel so that I can use it when granddad takes me to the river on Sunday."

Steve looked at his son closely; he looked so much like his mother that it still took him by surprise at how so alike they were. "And how much is this new reel going to cost?"

Alex leaned into his father's chest and replied in an almost whisper, "It's twenty-two pounds."

Steve felt the disappointment in his son's answer. He thought for a moment, then took Alex by the arms and gently teased him away, so he could see his face, "That's a lot of money for a fishing reel, Alex …"

Alex glanced away from his father's gaze, "Yeah, I know, Dad, but it really is a good reel … and granddad's always saying that I could catch more if I had a decent reel." He looked back at his father, the hint of tears in his eyes.

Steve sighed deeply and pulled Alex to him again and gave him a hug. "Hey hey … no need for tears." He felt Alex's arms reach around his waist and fought back his own wish to cry.

The bond between father and son was strong; it had grown in strength over the past ten years as they each grew together.

Steve cleared his throat and kissed Alex's head, "OK, so granddad thinks you are a great river fisherman does he?" Alex nodded again. "Well, we can't disappoint him then can we? But …" he paused as a plan formulated in his head, "… but, you're going to have to work for this, Alex …" Alex started to smile which took his father by surprise. "What?" he asked, "What have I said to make you smile?"

Alex's smile broadened. "Granddad said you'd make me work for it and I've already started."

Steve stared in amazement. "Started what?" he asked.

"Granddad said you'd probably get me to clear out the shed as part of a deal for you to buy me the reel and I started two days ago—I started cleaning the shed." Steve slumped back in his chair, staring at Alex. Alex went on, "I've already got those old bike frames out and I've put the garden tools back on their hooks and I've brushed all the cobwebs away ..." he paused for a breath, "but they keep coming back—the cobwebs."

Steve laughed. "Of course they will, it's home for the spiders and every time you brush them away, they have to rebuild ... building their webs so they can catch flies and insects, so they can survive."

Alex grinned. "Oh I know that, it's just ..."

Steve leaned forward and hugged him, "OK ... so you've started clearing the shed of spiders ... which, by the way, is a battle you will never win and granddad suggested that that was what I would ask you to do ... well, he was right—as usual—so you finish the shed and *if* I'm satisfied with the end result, I'll buy the reel for you. Is that a deal?"

Alex hugged harder. "Thanks Dad, you won't be disappointed, that old shed will look like new by the time I'm finished." They held each other for a while, lost in their own thoughts.

"OK, time for bed, young man," Steve said softly, "and don't forget, I'll be late home tomorrow, I'm going to the cemetery."

He felt Alex tense in his arms. "Yeah, I know." Alex pulled away and headed for the door and just as he was about to leave he turned slowly and said, "Dad ... will you tell Mum I love her too."

Instantly Steve's hand went to his mouth stifling

the cry. "Of course I will son ... of course I will—she knows you love her, she sees it every day in all the things you do."

Alex turned back to the door and pulled it open slowly, then turned again. "Will you tell her ..." his voice broke, "... will you tell her I miss her too."

Steve leapt from his chair and swept him up into his arms, "I know you miss her son, we all do." He hugged Alex tight against him, his mind racing back to the time when Alex was born and how he had lost the woman he had married just three short years before.

Alexandra had died in a freak accident a month after Alex was born. His mind went over those last few hours with her in the hospital; how she had almost begged Steve to take the love she had for him and her new son, to share that love with their son and how he was to 'live on' without her. Tears were stinging his eyes and he hugged his precious son closer. Her last words to him as she passed, whispered in his heart, *"Our little boy needs you now ... and please don't worry, I'll always be watching—both of you—I love you Steve Appleton and I'm sorry I have to go—leave."* He remembered her deep sigh as that last word fell from her lips—then she was gone.

As though his son was reading his mind, Alex spoke softly, "Is she watching Dad—is Mum watching us ... really I mean?"

Steve knelt and stood Alex in front of him. "You know ... I think she is. I think she watches over us every day and misses us, as much as we miss her." He answered, "Now, off to bed, it's late and you don't want to be late for school in the morning."

Alex stared at his father for a moment then gave a weak smile, turned and left, closing the door softly behind him. Steve watched him go, pride filling his heart.

When he returned to his desk he felt sure he was not alone in the room, he felt Alexandra there with him, her arms wrapped around his shoulders, her warm breath on his neck as she whispered, "Let me go Steve, please—Alex needs a mother and you need someone—I'll always be here and I know you will always love me but you have to live Steve, you have to live your own life—for the sake of our son." He crumpled over his desk, his heart breaking—he missed her so much. As the minutes passed, an image of somebody he'd seen recently filtered into his mind. She was, he'd thought, a good-looking woman, somebody he had seen at work as the image grew clearer. She had jet black hair, slim, about five feet tall and smiling eyes … suddenly he pushed back from his desk as though struck by lightning. Why had she come into his thoughts? Was it Alexandra? He sat motionless as more details of this woman began to clear in the mist of his mind. He remembered when he'd first seen her; a corridor at work, when he had held the door open for her and she'd thanked him. He remembered how he had watched as she continued down the corridor, admiring the way she carried herself. There was a confidence in the way she walked, something he recognised in his late wife. Her eyes were captivating, bright, something else he recognised about Alexandra. He stood and started to pace around the room, his thoughts in conflict; he couldn't consider replacing Alexandra with a replica; it would be wrong. He slumped down into his chair and allowed his thoughts to adjust to the prospect of meeting her—this stranger who worked at the same place he did. He began to smile as he admitted to himself that she was good-looking—elegant and attractive.

*

Alex woke early on Saturday morning and was already dressed when his father finally came down to the kitchen. The table had been set with all the breakfast things, toast was still warm in the rack and the teapot was covered with a floral cosy made for them by Brenda, mother-in-law and grandmother. Steve smiled a thank you to Alex, pulled a chair and sat down, leaning over and taking a slice of toast, placing it on his plate. He picked up the teapot and poured, noting it was strong, just as he liked it.

He looked over to Alex. "Well? Aren't you having breakfast?" Alex quickly sat down and grabbed a slice of toast. Steve could see the excitement in his son's face, "So …" he began, "when we've finished here, we'll go and take a look at the shed—OK?" Alex nodded eagerly, his mouth too full to speak. Steve's smile broadened as he'd already seen the work his son had done on the shed and was more than impressed, but for the sake of keeping to the agreement, was going through the motions of inspection and, if he was being really honest with himself, he wanted to share in the boy's excitement at knowing he'd worked for something he wanted—a new fishing reel.

Steve struggled to keep Alex under control as they approached the market, tightening his grip on his hand, making sure he didn't just run off. "So, where's the tackle man?" Steve asked.

Alex was pointing to the far corner. "He's over in

the corner ... can I go on and look please, Dad?" Alex asked, his excitement growing.

Steve strained to see lifting up on his toes, "OK, I see him." he said and gently jerked Alex to get his full attention. "Now, keep in my sight and do not run ... OK?"

Alex smiled, widely. "OK Dad ... thanks." He leaned up and kissed his father's cheek then turned and walked, almost running, in the direction of the stall. Steve watched as Alex dodged in between shoppers and chuckled when he ducked under the linked hands of a young couple who seemed to be pulling one another in opposite directions to show them something they'd seen on opposite stalls.

The tackle man was in deep conversation with two women when Alex got there so he began scanning for the reel—his new reel. He saw it and leaned forward and picked it up.

"Hey! Be careful with that, sonny," the stallholder barked, startling Alex and dropped the reel. The women turned to see who the stallholder was warning and when the taller one saw the look on Alex's face she moved forward, picked up the reel and handed it back to Alex.

"Here you go, nothing broken." She turned to the stallholder, "He'll be OK, he's got a good eye for a good reel," she said and looked back at Alex, noting a kind of familiarity of face that she just couldn't put her finger on. "That's a very fine reel by the way," she said. "I had one similar when I was younger." Alex looked up at the lady, astonishment on his face, as he'd never known women to go fishing. The lady smiled, recognising the questioning look. "Oh don't look so surprised, my dad always took me fishing whenever he could; we'd sit on the bank for hours … it was great fun."

Alex smiled. "My granddad takes me and he's promised to take me tomorrow morning … early." He glanced at the reel then back to the lady. "My dad might come too, though," he added.

The lady smiled. "So, you like to fish?" she asked.

Alex looked up again then glanced over his shoulder as old warnings from his father crept into his head about talking to strangers. "Yes I love to fish and—my dad's right here now." His smile grew and the lady again felt strange, as though she recognised him from somewhere.

"Well, good morning, Sally, I never knew you were into fishing. I hope my son Alex isn't bothering you."

Sally froze, the voice sending cold shivers down her spine and she couldn't stop herself from smiling. She looked up into the eyes of Steve Appleton. "Oh … good morning," she replied trying to catch her breath. "He's no bother—no bother at all—he's … just perfect." Her heart skipped a beat and she blushed, but she didn't care; she had already begun to wonder—hope—perhaps her 'happily ever after' was about to come true.

----- ~ -----

Visitors

I could hear something, a voice I think; it was very low, like a whisper, yet somehow I just knew, felt, it was asking me things, questions; it might have been coming from a great distance, I couldn't tell. I tried to answer but it felt as though my tongue had been glued to the roof of my mouth. It was dark too, although I think I saw the outline of some chairs and a table nearby. I know this all sounds a bit far-fetched, but I felt like I was in a kind of bubble; the surface was frosted and I couldn't see clearly, as though somebody had put a hood over my head.

When I tried to concentrate on the voice or noise or whatever it was, I seemed to freeze; not a cold freezing, more like I couldn't move. I couldn't move my arms and I couldn't move my legs; I couldn't even turn my head when I heard another sound coming from a different direction. I was scared. I do remember closing my eyes tight shut, but all that did was make things worse. It got darker and the noise or voice just stopped; I couldn't hear anything at all. So, when I relaxed a bit, it was a bit lighter and the noise/voice came back … albeit faintly.

I know I was feeling hot too; I could feel the sweat running down the side of my body. Actually, it was a single line of sweat running from under my right arm down to my waist. I tried to rub it dry through my shirt but my arm froze. I felt very uncomfortable because of my sweating; I became very conscious of 'not being alone' and I was sweating, which made me feel quite ... vulnerable, I suppose. I started to panic. My heart began to pound; I could feel it in my ears but it didn't block out the voice. I started to feel dizzy ... I think. I could feel a breeze, a wind on my face, it made me squint. It felt as though it was coming from my left side and I tried to turn away but I froze ... again. My breathing became very rapid and I had a strange taste in my mouth; the only way I can describe it is that it was like metal coffee or tea, you know? Like when you drink tea from a tin mug, it has that slight 'metallic' tangy taste to it. When I swallowed, to take the taste away, I nearly threw up.

*

The lady doctor was sitting across from me and had a large writing pad balanced on her knee. She was asking questions and I was giving my best answers. I noticed how she had to steady the pad with her other hand whenever she wrote something down. The small table in front of her had three cups on it and each cup was full of hot coffee. I had already decided to remain still, never moving, no matter what either of them said. I was rigid in my position, in both mind and body; they were never going to get through. Though there was one time when I put my hands in front of my face and looked at her through the tiny gaps between my fingers; she looked blurred ... no defined edges.

When she asked a question that made me think carefully before answering, I would tense up. I could feel my muscles going tight, as though they were automatically going rigid. Then after, when I had thought of the best answer, I'd relax, just a bit. I refused to say anything to the other person in there with us ... I didn't even acknowledge the fact that he was there, although he did say quite a bit.

She had bright red varnish on her fingernails that I thought was very 'outlandish' for her medical profession at least. She had long black hair that was loosely tied into some form of 'swirl thing' at the back of her head and she was continually brushing away stray strands from her face every time she looked down. I wondered how she managed to stay focused on her task. She also had very deep blue eyes ... very inquisitive eyes, unrevealing eyes; the sort you could look into for hours and never know what was going on behind them ... in her head. I kind of liked that about her; it was a challenge ... to see if I could work her out before she could me. Although it was an unfair challenge if you thought about it, because I already knew everything about me, and I was the one in control; I was in control of everything and anything she would ever possibly learn about me. I liked that idea ... being in control.

I started to get a headache; the nagging kind, the ones that start at the back of your head and quickly move to your temples and affect your eyes ... migraine I think. I've had them before and I've learnt how to control them; I simply squeeze, my eyes tight shut and in minutes they've gone. They do make me sweat though; not a lot, but enough to make me feel uncomfortable ... especially in company. I'm not in control of that ... yet. I'm learning though because every time I get one and I squint, then comes the sweating; I start to feel as though I'm spinning around, like a top, and I can't breathe very easily; my heart starts to thump and

I can feel it in my ears. The best cure I've found is coffee but drinking that makes my stomach heave. I picked up the cup from the table and took a big mouthful.

Those sneaky bastards … I'm sure they put some kind of drug in it, it tasted terrible, it was like drinking a mixture of coffee with iron filings instead of sugar. I tried to spit most of it away but I'd already swallowed a lot before I realised … they've done it before.

*

This is going to sound really strange too, but I started to feel sleepy and awake at the same time. I could feel my whole body relaxing and I could breathe more easily. The light in the centre of the ceiling wasn't hurting my eyes as much either and I could finally move my arms and legs. Somehow, I knew that if I just let 'things' happen I'd feel much better and be back to my old self again.

*

Male voice: *"Doctor Meredith, I think we have Sarah-Louise back."*
Female voice: *"Good … good … leave her to come through … let it happen naturally."*
Several minutes pass, patient closely monitored.
Male voice: *"It's not working doctor … we're losing her again."*
Female voice: *"Damn it … we nearly had her then; we'll have to increase the meds that's all. OK, give it half an hour and we'll try again."*

*

I have gone through this before. It's hard to explain really. I know when it's about to start because I start to feel anxious, stressed. I get tunnel vision; it's like looking through an old tube of Smarties. I see things too. I call one of those things the Invisible Black Rat. It's the first thing I 'see' from the corner of my eye when the anxiety starts; it's like a thin black rat that runs along the skirting boards of whatever room I'm in at the time. If there are no boards then it runs along the edge where the floor meets the walls and when I try to look directly at it, it disappears. It's very quick; I've watched it, from the corners of my eyes many times; it never seems to stop, just runs and runs ... round and round but ... it never goes up the walls, which I think is very strange. If it's a black rat, then it would be logical to think that it is searching for an escape and there are nearly always windows, it could quite easily escape through one of them.

The next stage of 'it' starting is when I get the feeling that I'm not on my own ... even though I am. I feel as though somebody else is with me ... somebody I can't see ... somebody watching me, listening and watching. I don't like that feeling and I can't seem to control it either; it just takes over and that's when I feel trapped ... trapped inside that bubble again.

----- ~ -----

Payback

Josh had never been a wealthy man, but for as long as he could remember, he had always helped those less fortunate than himself. He donated regularly to charities and made pledges to the variety of television appeals. He knew he could be somewhat self-indulgent in what he did, but he also knew—he would never stop. One of his 'pet' acts of kindness was to pay for things for complete strangers then—simply walk away. It had started accidentally; he was on a day trip to the beautiful village of Broadway in Worcestershire. After spending time wandering around the village, dropping into the various shops, he decided he'd have an early lunch, so he found a nice café and, whilst waiting for his sandwich to arrive, struck up a conversation with a couple who had taken the table next to his. He found out that they too were day-tripping, and that it was part of a birthday treat for the man from his wife. When Josh asked how old the gentleman was, he was astounded to be told that he was in his late 80's, since the man didn't have the look of somebody of such a great age. During their chatting, the idea of paying for their lunch as some kind of 'birthday gift' first started to manifest itself in his head. Since that day, he'd often asked himself why he'd done it, but had long since given up trying to rationalise the fact. As he was actually paying for their lunches, a thought struck him of how they might react when they came to make payment only to be told that it had been taken care of—in fact, to date, that had been the one and only time he'd stuck around to see how they had reacted.

As he left the café, making his way to the door, he stopped and wished the pair a good afternoon and the man another birthday wish of continued good health. Outside, he quickly crossed the road and dived inside a gift shop where he could see the doorway of the café. He felt slightly uncomfortable standing and watching, waiting for the couple to emerge, and when they finally came out he saw how they were looking up and down the street, obviously searching for the stranger who'd paid for their lunch. A feeling of guilty uncomfortableness grew inside him as he watched them from his hiding place—behind a tall pillar of postcards displayed just inside the shop. A deeper surge of guilt wracked him when he saw the telltale signs of consternation appear on their faces as they walked slowly away from the café towards the village green. It was then he vowed never to wait again.

On the coach home, he found he was struggling with his emotions about what he'd done; how he'd felt about himself for paying such a small sum of money for two complete strangers—how it had given him a 'buzz'— a good feeling inside. Throughout the journey, the more he thought, the more he felt less guilty about it and, by the time he'd reached the comfort of his home, he had come to a final and firm decision—he would do it again but would never stick around to see how his beneficiaries reacted.

*

About a month later, he was out shopping in the market town of Tewkesbury in Gloucestershire, a place he knew well and always enjoyed being there. The day had started bright, although the sunshine had become hidden behind thickening grey cloud as the morning wore on and it was a sudden downpour of heavy rain that had caught him, and most of the other people in the town, off guard. He didn't fancy the idea of wandering around the extensive market in damp clothes and decided to go and get a hot drink at one of the local cafés. He chose one he had been in before, a place where the atmosphere was always pleasant and the hosts friendly and approachable. It was the kind of place where he could sit and 'people-watch' and where he had often thought he could carry out one of his 'good deeds', although he knew he would have to be careful because the place was almost always full and he wondered if he could actually get away without being caught. Pushing open the door, he glanced up backwards at the sky and the black clouds gave no indication as to when the rain would stop which, he thought, would give him ample time to suss out his beneficiary of the day; he would study hard and make a decision based on all of his criteria of merit.

He placed his order and, whilst waiting, he'd given the place the 'once-over', finding he'd already singled out a number of possibilities. He sat himself down at an empty table—the only empty table near the stairs that led to more seating and tables, his rationale being that staying on the ground floor would give him plenty of time to 'do the deed' and then be able to make a quick exit.

When settled, he reached over to the sideboard that had advertisements for various local events and charities. He picked up a magazine to 'not' read whilst he made his decisions; the perfect disguise, he thought, a kind of undercover operation for him and something none of the other customers would suspect.

With the magazine, he *wasn't* reading, perched in his lap and resting on the table's edge, he sat listening and occasionally glancing up to take in more of the snippets of conversation going on around him. He kept his gaze averted so as not to attract attention until he heard the commotion of somebody coming in from the rain. He saw a young lady struggling to get a pushchair through the doorway and everybody seemed to be looking in the same direction—his, since his chair seemed to be closest to the front.

He felt a sudden surge of annoyance and frustration when he saw two young men sitting at the table on the opposite side of the café, close to the door, sniggering at the young mother's plight. He went over to help her. "Here, let me help," he said loudly; an attempt to embarrass the two younger men but it had no effect. Taking hold of the buggy and with a combination of pulls and pushes, he manoeuvred the buggy into the café.

"Oh … oh, thanks," the young lady replied, "… this is one of a few places that allows buggies and we've got soaked, haven't we Toby?" she continued. Josh gave her and the small boy a smile.

"You're welcome," he said, turning to go back to his table.

"I'm all wet, Mummy … I'm all wet," the small boy whined; his voice was quite shrill and lots of faces turned to see what was happening. "I'm all we-e-e-t," he continued loudly.

Josh turned to the table next to the door and paused

momentarily, glaring at the two men sitting there, wanting to say something but turned back to the mother and boy, smiled again and went back to his table.

He settled back to his 'task at hand' and picked up his magazine; one of three elderly ladies sitting at the table next to his leaned over and said in a loud whisper, "It's so nice to see there are still some gentlemen left in this world of ours." Josh looked over to her and saw the slightest of nods towards the two young men at the other table; he nodded his acknowledgement, smiled, then went back to *'not'* reading the magazine.

"Oh, I think it's a generational thing," another of the ladies said, in an equally loud whisper.

Josh tried to keep his head down but felt the first blushes filling his cheeks; he had never been one to simply accept a compliment.

Just as he began to feel comfortable with his surroundings, the young lady came over to his table. "I'm sorry to disturb you again, but there's no other tables free … could I—could we share yours … please?"

Josh quickly glanced around the café; he wanted to be left alone, but realised that would prove to be almost impossible. "Sure," he said with a warm smile and moved his cup unnecessarily away from the middle of the table closer to him. "Help yourself," he continued, leaning back slightly in an effort to give her more room to put whatever she needed out onto the table.

He watched as she settled herself into the chair opposite him whilst pulling the other chair closer to her— away from him and sat Toby down. He didn't know if he felt the gesture to be an insult or compliment and smiled awkwardly when she looked over at him.

"Thank you again for helping," she said with a warm smile, "it's nice knowing that there are still some gentlemen left in this town." She held his gaze for a while longer, making him feel more embarrassed.

"You're welcome," he replied, quickly glancing over to the older ladies, then down to his magazine, desperate to hide the blush that was filling his cheeks and, as he did so, he just caught a glimpse of their collective smiles.

Trying his best to concentrate on his task, but also knowing it was an ill-fought battle, he found himself listening to the whispered conversation between the young mother and her boy, Toby. "I know sweetheart, I know I said that but … listen, I promise to get you some the next time." She sounded desperate and embarrassed, not wanting to advertise her predicament as Toby insisted that he have whatever she had promised. She leaned in close to the boy and Josh could just make out what she was saying: "I'm sorry, Toby, but I haven't the money today for drinks and cake … I'll buy you some chocolate cake the next time … I promise."

Josh almost felt the plea in her voice and saw that she was beginning to get flustered. He listened more intently as she repeated her promise to the boy but Toby was having none of it.

"You always say that. We never have chocolate cake," he replied, a little too loudly for her liking.

He watched as her cheeks filled to a deep crimson and quickly looked away when she looked up at him. He felt sorry for her but knew his decision was made; he would treat them to their drinks with the addition of large slices of chocolate cake.

He finished his drink and began to stand. "Oh … I

hope we haven't disturbed you," the mother said, leaning forward, her voice quite low. Josh was taken aback momentarily, but quickly gained his composure. "Uh … oh … no, no, I have to go anyway." He fumbled his reply, smiled and made his way to the counter to pay. He approached the counter and deliberately stood in between the counter and the wall with his back to the rest of the café. The two ladies serving looked at him, seemingly questioning his encroachment into their workspace. He leaned forward and smiled as best he could to ease their discomfort and raised a finger to his lips in a gesture to keep their conversation secret. "I'd like to pay please," he began, "… but I'd also like to pay for the young lady and her son's—if I may." He found this bit of his task difficult because he knew that his well-intended gestures always hinged on the discretion of the proprietors.

The two ladies held his gaze a while and he started to pray they would catch on soon so he could do the deed and leave. He glanced nervously behind him then back to the two ladies, "… and the table with the—older ladies," he said in a low voice. He waited as the two ladies exchanged looks and then looked back at him.

Then one of them leaned forward slightly. "You want to pay for your table—your coffee, the drinks for the young lady and her boy—*and* the table next to them?"

Josh slowly nodded and smiled again. "Yes—please," he whispered.

The two ladies exchanged looks again and the second took a step towards Josh. "You want to pay for them …" —she waved her hand in front of her— "… all?" Her question sounded louder than it actually was to Josh but he simply nodded again.

"Yesss—all of them," he replied, reaching for his wallet. He took out his card and held it up. "Please, just take whatever is needed for the three tables … oh, and take for two, big slices of chocolate cake, for the mother and her boy as well please." He kept out his hand with the card, offering it from one to the other, almost insisting one of them take it. The first of the two stepped forward, gingerly took the card and again exchanged a look with her colleague.

"Uh, OK sir," she said and turned to the till. She picked up two slips of paper, glanced back at Josh and finally smiled. "Ah, I see …" she said softly and went back to the slips.

Josh breathed a deep, silent sigh of relief and looked around at the tables involved then back to the lady at the till. She was busy tapping at numbers on a small calculator. She turned round, stepped back to Josh and, in a low whisper said, "In total sir, that's twenty-three pounds and twenty-seven pence." She looked up at Josh who had raised an eyebrow, he hadn't expected it to be as much, which the lady obviously guessed. "The three ladies have had scones and teas and, with the added chocolate cake, the bill for the lady and her boy comes to …"

Josh raised his finger and smiled. "That's fine—it's OK, but what about my drink?" he asked.

The lady smiled warmly, "Well, sir, I've decided that if you're being such a Samaritan and paying for all of theirs, then yours should be free—on the house … our treat for you." Josh blushed, as this had never happened before, but he smiled graciously and thanked her, his shoulders relaxing as the transaction went through. He knew he was vulnerable at that particular moment and just wanted to leave. The lady brought the receipt with his card and, as she handed them to him she whispered, "Thank you sir; it really is good to know there are good, decent people around in this day and age and the next time you call in—your drinks will be free … OK?" Josh reached for his card and receipt but the lady held on to them, "Agreed?" she asked with a smile.

Josh nodded. "But will you recognise me—if I come back?" he said.

"Oh, I know you'll be back sir, you've been here many times and I've watched you … watching our other customers … and, if this is the result of your watching, then you'll always be welcome." She released her hold on the card and receipt giving Josh a wink. He blushed, again, and made his way out of the café.

Walking up the high street, he pulled his collar up against the drizzle, hesitating, wondering what it would be like to go back into that café and do the same again—or, going back and seeing the same people. It was a worry, but only a minor one; he smiled and carried on, gazing up to the sky, seeing the rain was finally easing.

----- ~ -----

A Second Time Around

In 1976, when Tom married Lizzie, they had both just turned eighteen and some had said it wouldn't last. Lizzie's mother actually asked her, on the morning of the wedding, if she was sure that it was what she wanted. Lizzie remembered vividly what she had said to her mother: "Mum, I am the happiest girl in the world because I know Tom will never hurt me or run off, whatever else people might think. We are in love and that's all that matters." The wedding itself was an occasion where everybody was full of hope and encouragement for the couple since it was such a whirlwind romance, having only known each other for less than two years.

After the first year or so, when there were signs that things were not as good as they appeared, whispers had started amongst those who had initially thought the worst, that Tom and Lizzie would separate and therefore fulfil their predictions. However, the pair had battled through and now, in 2016, plans were being made to celebrate their fortieth anniversary.

Lizzie had got used to the fact that, at every milestone of their anniversary, Tom made extra-special plans. On their tenth anniversary, he had booked a weekend at a very luxurious country hotel and had had ten red roses delivered to her the day before they left. She remembered how she had cried with joy at his show of love for her. On their twentieth, he had arranged a river cruise around Europe that had lasted almost two weeks and they enjoyed a wonderful time together.

It was their thirtieth that had been a bit flat; Tom had been involved in a car accident and suffered a head injury. The hospital had put him into a medically induced coma for ten days and, when he eventually regained consciousness, there were signs of minor memory loss. Lizzie had taken care of him when they said he was fit enough to go home and it had put a huge strain on her. In fact, it had taken a full two years for him to regain any kind of recognisable independence from her care and then be able to return to work. It was only after the accident that Lizzie found out about his plans to fly out to New York for a long weekend, 'a trip of a lifetime' is what he'd called it but they had lost their deposit when they couldn't go.

*

This year seemed to be no different from all the other milestone anniversaries. Lizzie was very much aware that Tom had once again begun to put together plans that involved travel and unknown expense, but she had made a decision of her own. This year, she was going to be the one who made the plans. It was going to be her secret they celebrated and she was not going to be put off—by anyone. She had already spoken with their daughter and son who had reluctantly agreed to forestall any and all 'little jobs' he would inevitably ask them to do for him under the proviso of 'not-telling-your-mother' because it was to be a surprise. Sarah, their daughter, had given back three cheques her dad had given to her to pay for flights, hotels and flowers and was quite upset at having to be so deceitful towards her father—until that is, when Lizzie reminded her that she had been complicit in the secret dealings for the New York trip.

There was one thing Lizzie had not thought about when she embarked on her little project, and that was how difficult it was proving to be at keeping things so secret from him. They had always shared everything in their lives and trying to do something so important, without him knowing or finding out, was quite scary at times. As far as she could remember, she had only been 'nearly' found out twice. The first was when she was making arrangements for the actual day everything was to come together. She was finalising things on the telephone when Tom came in unexpectedly; she had got all flustered and quickly put the phone down, without finishing the call. The feeling she got was the same as the one she had when her father caught her kissing a boy from school—she was all hot and bothered and had run straight to her room in utter embarrassment. This time, she couldn't just run to her room and hide; she had to endure the quizzical looks from Tom. She worried that he had figured everything out and was trying not to let on. The second time wasn't so much scary... more comical. Tom had seen her taking what appeared to be a note from Derrick, their son, and had asked what it was and they both gave very different explanations. Derrick had said it was just a receipt he'd found and Lizzie had said it was a recipe for hot cross buns or something. She had later found Tom searching through her pockets, no doubt looking for incriminating evidence.

*

The final phase of the operation was fast approaching and it was again proving difficult to give a plausible reason why Lizzie wanted Tom to put on his best suit for the day in question. It was Sarah who had had the brilliant idea of telling him that they had all been invited to a wedding by a distant niece or nephew. They had even bought some fancy invitations and had made up names to which he said, "The names sound familiar, although I can't actually remember them since that accident." Lizzie felt terribly guilty when he'd said that because she felt as though she was dragging back bad memories for him.

*

On the Friday, a week before their anniversary, Tom had come home from work in a mood. He'd had a call from their son telling him that his plans for the anniversary had had to be cancelled because of events surrounding flights to and from America. It was all over the news, terrorist threats had been made and the airline companies had grounded all international flights. Although Lizzie was pleased about Tom's plans being scuppered, she had to maintain a degree of indifference as to why he was so tetchy. The announcement had also helped her and the family to regain control of the whole anniversary situation.

On that Saturday morning, the sun rose in the sky and seemed brighter to Lizzie; she was hiding her panic well. She wanted this day to be the best. After visiting the hairdresser, she found Tom sitting in his chair oblivious of the time and the need to be getting himself ready. "Oh come on, Tom, we've got to get to the church."

Tom looked up and said, "Well Lizzie, to be honest, I don't remember the young lady—my niece, and it feels like we'd be intruding." He settled back in his chair.

Lizzie's panic rose, but she managed to keep her voice level and calm. "Don't be silly; besides, it would be very rude of us if we didn't turn up, especially since we've already sent back our RSVP."

Tom looked at her. "Yes I know but …" his voice trailed off.

Lizzie knelt down beside him. "What is it Tom? What's the matter?"

Tom turned his face away for a moment then back to hers. "I can't remember our wedding, Lizzie … no matter how much we've tried to jog my memory. Looking through the wedding albums, listening to family and friends, it's all gone, Lizzie, all gone and I hate it … I hate not being able to remember."

Lizzie stared at him for a moment, seeing the pain in his eyes. She took his hand and said, "I know, love, I know … but who knows, going to this wedding might somehow trigger something, you know … this might be just the kind of jolt your memory needs. The sounds, the smells … seeing faces you might recognise because you know all the family have been invited." She leaned in and hugged him.

The silence between them was deafening and she knew she would have to use all her powers to persuade him to go. A few moments passed then Tom cleared his throat. "I guess you could be right … as always."

Lizzie smiled to herself.

*

In the taxi, on their way to the church, Tom was very quiet and Lizzie knew he was still tormenting himself about the day ahead and of the fact that he couldn't remember their wedding and many of the things they did together when they were newly married. She reached over for his hand and squeezed it gently. "Everything is going to be all right Tom; please stop worrying yourself."

Tom looked at her and smiled. "I know … it's just that because I can't remember, I feel as though I've lost something, something very precious—for both of us." He leaned to her and kissed her cheek. "You have a knack of making things right for me, Lizzie, you know that don't you?"

Lizzie smiled, "And you do for me, my love."

At the gates to the church, they were met by their son Derrick and daughter Sarah, and Derrick took Tom by the arm and said they needed to get inside quickly because the bride was expected at any moment. Sarah stood next to her mother and made small talk about her outfit. Derrick led Tom to the front of the church and when inside he made straight for the altar. Tom was perplexed and started to protest when the organ started up with the tune of 'Here Comes the Bride'.

Derrick beamed at his father. "You need to turn around, Dad."

Tom, ever more confused, looked back down the aisle and caught his breath when he saw his Lizzie standing near to the last pew, her face covered by a white veil and a large posy of flowers in her hands, Sarah standing next to her smiling like the Cheshire Cat.

"What … what's going on?" Tom asked.

Derrick smiled and took a small step away. "You'd better ask Mum."

As the organ played, Lizzie and Sarah walked

sedately down towards Tom, both smiling as they watched Tom's face change from confusion to realisation. Derrick handed over a handkerchief and Tom wiped his eyes.

The vicar called for the congregation's attention, "Ladies and gentlemen, we are gathered here today to witness the re-joining of Tom and Lizzie in holy matrimony." He looked to Lizzie and nodded.

Lizzie turned to Tom, her voice soft and warm and said, "Tom, my darling husband, I have known for many years how you have suffered inside at the fact that you cannot remember the very first time we did this, so I and the family wanted to give you a day that you would remember and cherish. I want to marry you—again."

Tom stared at her, tears filling his eyes. "I said earlier that you have a knack of making things right for me—and you have really outdone yourself this time. I would love to marry you—again."

----- ~ -----

Discovery

It was a Friday evening and Claire had been sitting at her desk for more than twenty minutes studying the results of the latest batch of comparative tests. As far as routine tests went, these were no different but there was one result that stood out from the others. She tapped a key on her laptop and the whole image enlarged and she leaned forward to take a closer look. Sitting back, she felt a sense of disbelief. In all the years she had been doing these types of tests, she had never once encountered this form of result. She sighed, it was late and the lab was almost empty of colleagues or anybody with whom she could discuss the findings. Tapping the keypad again, the image reverted back to its original size and she hit the button for a printout of the results and sent the page to the department's printer. By the time she walked over to the printer, the system had produced a clear copy of what she had on her screen. She looked at it again, drew a circle around the puzzling result and went back to her desk where she placed the result inside a pocket folder with the sample tissue slivers. She checked her watch against the lab's wall-mounted clock and sighed deeply; finishing the report and sending it up was going to make her late again. She opened another window on her laptop and began typing up her report.

*

Monday morning and Brenda reread the report whilst taking another sip of hot coffee from her polystyrene cup; the highlighted findings were not what were expected and she made a mental note to give Claire a call and discuss it with her. The fact that her job as Lab Supervisor was to check the results of all tests carried out in her department, then forward them to whichever department had made the request was, quite simply pointless, since every department could access the data from any computer on the hospital system. The changes to protocol had been put into place almost two years ago after a near fatal error, a little over three years ago, had occurred and had attracted wide public interest from local and national news media. The results on this particular test had been requested by the Surgical Department for what she understood was a scheduled procedure later in the month and, although there was plenty of time, she decided to call Moira in Surgical to give her the results and let her deal with it. She picked up her phone and punched in the extension number from a printed list tacked to a clipboard hanging on the wall above her desk. She closed the file with the samples attached whilst she waited for her call to be answered.

*

Moira was speaking on the phone when Colin Turvey and his guest entered her office and she raised her hand to ensure he didn't leave, pointing to the handset against her ear; he nodded his understanding and waited. The long silence from Moira made him more curious about the call. "Yep, yep OK, thanks Bren', I'll talk to you later OK?" Moira said, then put the phone back onto its cradle. She looked at the notes she'd made in her notebook then looked up at Colin, "We have a bit of a …" she paused, searching for the correct word, "… shall we call it, a situation, Mr Turvey." She finished and acknowledged his guest with a slight nod of her head.

Colin Turvey looked at her. "What do you mean Moira? A situation … in respect of what?"

Moira stood and picked up the notebook. "It's to do with your procedure scheduled for the twenty-eighth; she picked the folder off her desk and flipped it open and read the names, Young and Lander, we've got the results of the latest tests and there seems to be something of a … an anomaly." She handed him a copy of the results and watched as he studied them. "The samples will be with us later," she continued.

Colin Turvey was the Senior Surgical Clinician and a revered teacher at the University Hospital. He flipped the pages back and forth, his eyebrows dancing across his forehead as he read, a habit he had acquired over the years and something he always did whilst reading; it was also the source of many humorous comments behind his back.

He blew out his cheeks, "Well, well, didn't see that coming did we, eh?" he said, his question not aimed at anyone in particular. He smiled at Moira and handed the report to his guest. "Here, you're the forensic expert; tell me what you see and think of those."

Whilst his guest read through the text he continued to talk with Moira. "This is Sara Mundie; she's our guest speaker at this evening's lecture / dinner; top man, as it were, of forensics and works with the Metropolitan Police all the time … finding bad guys and whatnot through DNA and other materials left behind at crime scenes … all very exciting, eh?" He smiled broadly and hunched his shoulders like a small child trying desperately to hold back his excitement.

After reading through the report, Sara handed the results sheets back to him. "Actually, Colin, they do look rather interesting, wouldn't mind digging a little deeper later, if you don't mind, obviously … and if it's within legal limits etcetera."

Colin turned to Moira. "Oh I'm sure we can allow that, can't we Moira? Do you have an extra copy for Sara to take away with her and study?"

Moira sat back down, adjusted the position of the laptop slightly before hitting 'Ctrl P' on the keypad and almost instantly the printer delivered the pages. Reaching over, Moira took them out of the tray, checked them through, then handed them to Mr Turvey.

"Thank you," he almost whispered and ushered Sara out of the office.

*

Sara walked into the lobby of the lab building on Thursday morning. She nodded to the security officer who was sitting behind a tall reception desk and carried on past to the little corridor where the lifts were. She was searching through her holdall for the keys to her office and found the report she had been given by Colin Turvey on Monday. She flipped the buff folder open and glanced at the result diagram quickly, trying to reignite the thoughts that had made her ask for a copy in the first place. She pulled the top page off and instantly saw what she had seen before; questions began filling her head immediately and she prayed silently that the samples that accompanied the report had arrived.

She dropped her bag to the side of her desk and picked up the small package with the University Hospital stamp emblazoned along the top left corner and, together with the folder in hand, went straight to her leading technical analyst, Alan.

"Good morning Alan, what are you working on this morning?" she asked.

He looked up and smiled. "Good morning 'boss-lady', enjoy your dinner at the Uni then?"

Sara smiled back. "It was what could be called an interesting and intellectual evening ... nothing like some of the nights we share in here." She looked at the papers on his desk, flipping the pages but not really taking any interest in them; she knew he was finishing off the report findings of another murder for the Met Police. He watched her closely.

"CPS needs the final for the end of the month," he said when she returned the pages to where he'd left them.

"Good. Will you do your favourite 'boss-lady' a huge favour when you've got a spare five minutes or so?" She tilted her head slightly and gave Alan a bigger smile. "Pleeease."

He stared at her for a moment, then saw the folder and parcel in her hand. "Oh I get it; another project, eh? Nothing official ... just run the checks and tests and come tell you, eh?"

She put her arm around his shoulders and hugged him; he took off his glasses and dropped his head to his chest in submission looking up at her sideways. "OK, OK ... what do you have this time?"

She dropped the folder on top of the file, opened the

cover and tapped the first page. "Look at that and tell me what you see," she said.

He put his glasses back on and looked down at the front page and began to read. After a few moments, he looked up, removed his glasses again but said nothing. He leaned forward to recheck what he'd just read, squinting at the jumble of words, numbers and black blotches.

"Put your glasses on," Sara said, nudging him with her elbow, "you'll damage your eyes reading like that."

Alan let out a slight grunt. "It's a bit late for that, my eyes are already shot from looking through magnified glass in the microscopes all day long." He slipped the lenses over his eyes, holding them in place, and leaned in closer to the diagram. Sara sensed his interest and leaned in closer too.

"What do you see?" she asked in a low voice.

"Shadow!" Alan announced, sarcastically.

Sara straightened up and patted him gently on the shoulder. "OK, will you do it for me Al? I'll be in meetings most of the morning, but would love to come away knowing that you've found …"

Alan turned to her removing his glasses from his face. "Have I ever refused you, boss-lady?" He glanced at the pages on his desk, then back to Sara. "It'll take a while, but … yes, I should be able to get something for you by noon, maybe one o'clock." She tapped his arm again then left him to his work.

Sara slumped down into her chair behind her desk and kicked off her shoes scrunching her toes a few times. She hated having to attend admin meetings where she had to justify the running of her department, the manpower, resources and costs etc., and although she was fully aware that they were a necessary evil of running a business, she found them time-consuming and boring. She looked at her watch, it was a little after twelve thirty, and she needed fresh coffee and a bite to eat as her stomach had been growling for most of the morning. As she leaned down to put her shoes on again she saw the single sheet of blue tinted paper set next to her telephone. She tried to read the scrawling handwritten note whilst tapping around the floor for her shoes. She knew the note was from Alan, as no one else in the lab had handwriting like his, and she gave up on the shoes when she read the words 'match' and 'flagged'. Sitting up, she picked up the page and read the note again:

'S, ran checks and did secondary epithelial, DNA. Near-perfect match, result flagged historical num. #553347/CPH. Interesting. Need to speak. A.'

Sara dropped the paper, found her shoes and headed to the lab. She found Alan sitting to the side of his desk, bent forward, reading. He appeared oblivious to his surroundings; he held a sandwich box in one hand and a bottle of still water in the other, both of which were being ignored. As Sara approached, he blinked and raised his hand with the sandwich box. "Here, you need these more than I do."

Sara was always amazed at how his senses worked; she took the sandwich box, opened it and selected a small, round soft bun and bit into it. She knew its filling was fresh salmon and finely chopped onion blended together with a dash of squeezed lemon and extra virgin olive oil—Alan had salmon, onion and virgin oil sandwiches every day, although he would add a little coriander every now and then just to spice things up. Sara was not a fan of the delicate aromatic herb and was pleased to find that this was not one of those days.

"Incredible, absolutely incredible," he said to himself, "… absolutely, fascinatingly incredible," he continued.

Sara leaned forward, her mouth full of sandwich. "Mm … what is it?" she asked.

Alan paused and half turned his head towards her, "That smell of lemon mixed with olive oil … it gives you a sense of being in far-off Portugal, where they gently cook sardines fresh from the sea on griddles and drip lemon oil over the burning skins …" Sara nudged him in the ribs and he feigned being deeply injured.

"What are you reading?" she said, before taking another bite of the delicious bread roll.

Alan looked up at her and smiled, "This story is incredible."

"Yes, I've gathered that much, you've said it four times already."

"Case #553347/CPH details the brief that nine years ago there was an accident where several souls lost their lives; terrible accident, happened on the M25 motorway, thick fog, etc. Well, in one of the cars was a family; mum, dad and a small, very young child; parents lost their lives, but the little kid survived. According to statements from Social Services, etc., the grandparents were either unable, or unwilling—take your pick—to take on the responsibility of a newborn, hence baby being put up for adoption." He looked at Sara. "You following all this?" She nodded and poked the last of her sandwich into her mouth. Alan continued with his narrative, "OK, well obviously the child got better and was fostered and eventually adopted." He angled the file so Sara could read the last paragraph for herself.

*

Colin Turvey was sitting behind his large mahogany desk with three single printed pages in front of him and was pushing and pulling at them in order as he spoke. "Yes, right, I first of all want to thank you both, Mr and Mrs Young, for coming in and I apologise for any sense of secrecy or deception you may have felt, but I can assure you that what I'm about to tell you, will, I think, be a bit of a shock for you. I can honestly say it was for all of us here at the hospital; indeed; a colleague of mine claimed it to be a one in a million chance of ever happening. However, before I give you the news, I would like to clarify some facts. After you married, you found that you were unable to become natural parents and so decided to adopt; you were introduced to young Charlie and, in time, were successful in adopting him. Then, a little over two years ago, he was diagnosed with a very rare condition that we've discovered to be 'Congenital hypoplastic anaemia' and is in desperate need of bone marrow transplantation. With searches, no suitable donors were found until Andrew requested to be tested; those tests were carried out last Friday afternoon." He looked at the last page of the three in front of him, lifted it from his desk and studied it, then slowly replaced it in line with the others. He looked at the two people sitting in front of him and a broad smile formed on his face. "I am pleased to say, Andrew, you are a near-perfect match, which is not only excellent news for young Charlie, but I rather hope it would strongly suggest that you are, in fact, his natural father."

----- ~ -----

'Author ... Author'

She looked up at the clock above the fireplace; four minutes had passed since she'd last looked, although it seemed much longer; she silently swore at herself. She knew that she had power—the power of controlling her time, but she was still putting herself under enormous pressure and, on top of that, one single thought crept back into her head: 'this has to be finished—today'.

Swivelling in her high-backed leather chair, she stood and stretched. She was tired and knew that even though she was reaching for the ceiling, she would never touch it; the ceilings were high in the house and everything in it was new. She slumped back into the chair, exhausted from doing something actually physical; then, with a very basic calculation, worked out that it had been more than five months since she'd done any form of physical exercise, with the exception of getting up from her chair, making coffee or something to eat, then going back to sitting at her desk—to do more work. She thought for a moment and decided that what she really needed was fresh air and another coffee; something to stimulate her, so she climbed out of the chair and headed for the kitchen, knowing full well that what she really wanted was a cigarette. As she entered the farmhouse-style kitchen, she knew in her heart that completion of her task was literally at her fingertips and swore again when she realised that she'd looked at the huge kitchen clock on the wall near to the Aga range. Flipping the switch of the kettle, she instinctively reached over to the side and picked up the pack of cigarettes and small silver lighter, stuffing them in her pocket, and went to the French doors. Opening them with a flourish, she stepped out onto the raised decking, standing for a moment, then closing her eyes she breathed in deeply, filling her lungs with as much fresh air as she could; life for her had changed and she was determined to enjoy every last second.

She jumped when the shrill sound of the telephone rang and spun around staring at the pure white piece of technology hanging on the opposite wall and very nearly went back to answer, but stopped herself. She knew who would be calling and did not want to continue telling lies, whether they were little white ones, or huge great whoppers. She continued to stare at it, willing it to stop but it appeared that even her psychic powers had deserted her. She tried blocking out the sound of electronic bells, but they seemed to penetrate through her skull with the precision of a surgeon's knife and she eventually took a step forward, but the ringing stopped just as suddenly as it had started. With a heavy sigh, she allowed her shoulders to drop then slowly turned back around to face the garden. She wanted to relax; to have at least ten, maybe thirty or so minutes to herself where she could simply sit and let the world exist without her for a while—she needed that cigarette.

Stepping further out onto the decking, she turned her face to the sun and closed her eyes again, feeling its warmth and energy of life returning to her, and rummaged in her pocket for her cigarettes. It had always fascinated her that she could have her eyes closed, or be somewhere where the light was dim or even blacked out, yet still be able to locate the smallest of objects hidden deep in her pockets, and she smiled when she pulled out the slim packet and lighter. With that seemingly simple task achieved, she walked over to one of the new patio chairs and sat herself down into its plump cushioned seat and placed the pack and lighter on the equally new glass-topped table next to the large pink-smoked coloured ashtray. She counted the half-smoked butts and gave herself a 'self-congratulatory' slap on the back; there were only five butts, whereas only a few short weeks ago there would've been a whole lot more; then she rebuked herself for still being a smoker.

*

She'd only meant to close her eyes for a moment, but found she'd dozed for almost a whole half-hour and decided to wake herself up by walking around the garden —her garden. She'd kicked off her shoes and was walking on the lush lawn, squeezing her toes every now and then just to feel the soft grass as it tickled between them. The whole garden was neatly laid to lawn with deep flower borders on all sides. She had learned, slowly, the sometimes subtle difference in the fragrances of each plant as she passed by, occasionally stopping and lifting individual flower heads with their soft petals to her nose; and although she didn't know the names of all the flowers yet, she always felt relaxed and calm whenever she wandered around her beautiful sanctuary, taking in the sounds of nature. When she'd reached the bottom of the garden, she turned to look up to the house; it was a very large house, as wide as it was long and it still took her breath away—because all of it—every single brick, every window, every roof tile—and the garden—was hers. There was no mortgage or loan outstanding on any of it—it was all hers; bought and paid for from the sweat of her brow, the months of hard work and determined dedication; she sighed the sigh of absolute contentment then wandered over to the pine bench she'd commissioned in memory of her late mother and sat down. Memories flooding her mind of when things were tough—for her mother, a single parent of three children, two girls and a boy. She remembered fondly how her mother had always encouraged them all in whatever pursuit they had at any given time. She remembered the large writing book her mother had bought for her when she first started writing. She knew exactly where that book was—on her bedside table. It was something she would treasure for the rest of her life—especially as she remembered what her old English teacher, Mrs Elliot, had written when she left school:

> *'Never give up your writing, you are a natural talent and the world needs to see and experience your imagination because you can inspire a generation'.*

She would read the piece every night before going to sleep, remembering past times when she was struggling with life as a teenager and how she took great solace from Mrs Elliot who had helped her in ways that nobody could or would have. Then she would read the words her mother had written:

> *'Write with the love in your heart—I am so proud of you. All my love, Mum. xxx'*

She sighed again and gazed up towards the house, the different array of colours of the flower borders catching her eyes as they swayed gently in the breeze. She closed her eyes and took in the sounds of nature around her. She could hear the humming of bees busily going about their day; the chirps of other insects as they too went about their day. The different scents of flowers wafted around as the breeze swirled, bringing with it other distant sounds. Birdsong filled her ears and she slowly began to relax. Feeling the warmth of the sun on her face and the strain of the last few weeks drain from her body, she settled on the bench and allowed the serenity of the morning to wash over her.

As though mesmerised by her surroundings, she allowed herself the indulgence of a few moments of freethinking; something she did often. It was her way of releasing herself from the pressure she had put herself under; she would allow her mind to wander and not worry about what those thoughts meant. It wasn't long before the distant sounds of the nearby town filtered through and she pictured the bustle of the townsfolk as they went about their daily lives. She pictured in her mind the local traders and various shopkeepers hawking their wares; other businesses doing their best to look 'all-important' to their potential customers. She could imagine individuals making what they believed to be essential decisions about trivial matters but, nevertheless, significant to their lives.

She smiled to herself when she remembered something her mother had said many years ago: 'It is the female of the species that holds the power in the world; the wives of men make the important decisions in life because it is the women of the world who make the biggest differences to the world.' She also remembered watching the late evening news on television some years later where the world leaders were assembled in some summit meeting and they were making 'important decisions' through discussions and she'd pointed out to her mother that every single one of them was a man. She remembered her mother's smile when she said, "And you think that these men have not talked it through with their wives and asked for their opinions?"

A distant whistling sound drifted on the air and she remembered the kettle and sighed heavily as its sound reminded her of a heavy chain of responsibility dragging her back to work … but it was work she loved and a renewed sense of enthusiasm began to grow inside her, so she got up from the bench and strode confidently towards the house. She knew better than anybody how much her life had changed in the past three years; how she could indulge in the smallest of delights because her book—her very first book—had been a huge success which, in turn, had rewarded her with the luxuries she now enjoyed. Although she still remembered how difficult it had been to get her work published; the rejection letters and how her hopes and dreams slowly died as each one of them landed on her doorstep. But all of that was behind her and now she was in control of her future. A smile formed, contemplating what she had to do as she climbed up the three steps of the raised decking and in through the French doors. The fact that her book had shot into the top ten of the best sellers' list within weeks of being published and was still there, made her smile wider.

Her heart lifted as she poured boiling water over the coffee grains, then glanced at the clock. She'd been a little over-indulgent with her time in the garden but there was no real sense of panic; she was in absolute control of everything and headed back to her study.

Seated in her high-backed leather chair in front of her antique Victorian writing desk, she quickly read through what she felt was the final two chapters of her second novel. Her agent and publisher had agreed that what she had submitted so far was good work, but that it needed an ending fitting for the sequel she'd agreed upon. She already had the basics of the second part and was confident that whatever time constraints they put on her, she would 'come up with the goods' in plenty of time.

Satisfied with what she'd read, she opened her email account, attached the forty-something pages to the draft email she'd written at the start of the day, then deftly guided the cursor to the send icon and clicked the mouse button. She looked at the travel clock at the side of the desk and its hands told her it was 14:32; her smile broadened as she leaned back in the soft cushions of her chair.

----- ~ -----

Verdict

I knew the day was going to be difficult and, for the last half an hour or so, I'd been left to my own devices. Oh, don't get me wrong, I had help earlier but I felt so alone ... probably because I knew the whole day would be a strain—emotionally. It was only when I actually entered the courtroom that I felt like I was on display ... as though I had a bigger part to play in its proceedings than I'd realised—but I was in the public gallery. I suppose it was the size of the place that got me worried ... no, not worried—shocked. I thought it would have been much bigger, you know, like you see on the TV, with its wood panelling and subtle lighting, but this courtroom was a lot smaller, well, smaller than I had ever imagined.

From where I was sitting, I could see everything. The room did have wood panelling, but it was a light wood and highly polished ... in fact everything that was made of wood was the same. The tables, the floor and the handrails were all made up of this highly polished light-coloured wood; it was quite impressive really. The lights were those hidden types, you know, up behind frosted panels and they made the whole place seem almost too bright for what the place represented, law and justice. The thing that caught my eye the most was the huge crest high on the wall above the judge's chair, although I'm told it's called the judge's 'bench', but it looked just like a very expensive leather chair to me. The colours in the crest seemed to shine outwards and into every corner of the room—and I have to admit, it was magnificent. The intricate detail of it had me spellbound for ages. When I looked at the 'business' area of the room I could see that all the benches, where the 'legals' worked, was also of the same matching wood. I got the name 'legals' from someone who was talking with another person in the entrance hall on the first day I was here. And, from where I was, I could see the tops of the bannister-type rails, at the back of the benches, had been worn down and lost some of their sheen. I also noticed four very large speakers mounted in the corners of the ceiling, tilted down towards the centre of the room. I guess they were like that so that everybody would be able to hear, clearly, everything that was going on during a 'session'. I also wondered if they ever played music through them when the court was not being used for legal stuff.

I had no idea of how long I had been sitting there, but I got a strange feeling—like I was being watched—you know? A feeling that makes the hair on the back of your neck stand up and you get a tingly shiver go up and down your spine. So I looked around at all the different faces of the people in the room and most of them seemed to be either looking directly at me or from the corners of their eyes; it was quite off-putting. Some of them were wearing those long black robes that flowed majestically whenever they moved from one place to another and some were wearing those ridiculous white wigs that made them look so much older than they actually were. When they realised that I was looking back at them the same way they were looking at me, they quickly averted their stares and got back to their work … at least that's how it seemed to me. That's when I heard the cough.

*

I immediately turned my head in the direction of where the cough had come from and I looked straight into the eyes of a man who seemed familiar. He was sitting alone behind what I can only describe as what looked like a wall of wood panelling and glass. From where I was, I could see he was wearing a nicely tailored jacket, a white shirt with a yellow and red diagonally-striped tie. I must admit, he looked very handsome as well as familiar and something inside my head told me that his tie was tied in a full Windsor knot … and I have no idea why I would ever have thought about that. The more I looked at him the more I noticed. I could see his eyes were puffy and red, as though he'd been crying, but there was no evidence to support my thoughts. His darkish brown hair was cut short and swept back with a barely visible centre parting. I say his darkish brown hair but, in truth, there was a fair amount of grey flecked through it—and yes, he did look quite distinguished. I had no idea of his age, but I thought he looked a lot younger than he probably was and, when I realised he was looking straight back at me, I got all flustered—embarrassed even. Then a bell sounded from somewhere to my right and he turned his gaze away from me and, for a split second, I thought I'd embarrassed him.

*

I could hear lots of shuffling feet and chairs scraping on the floor and I remembered how I tried to cover my ears, but it only lasted a few moments so it didn't bother me that much. Then somebody called out in a loud voice for the court to come to order, which I thought was quite silly really because there weren't that many people in the room anyway.

I heard a door behind the judge's bench close. I'd heard it a couple of times before when I was in here the day before, I think, and from the corner of my eye I could see he was looking in my direction … he did that the first time I was in the courtroom. I thought he looked very regal in his bright-red robe and it was when he looked at me directly I turned away, but I don't know why; perhaps because I felt embarrassed again.

I continued looking the other way because again, from the corner of my eye, I could see him talking to a woman who was wearing one of those long, black robes. She was standing up next to the tall bench where the judge was sitting when she looked over in my direction and I just knew they were discussing something about me. Then I noticed how the silence in the whole courtroom seemed to get louder as the two of them talked. I could hear a kind of hissing in my ears just like when you are trying to go to sleep at night; everything is so quiet that you can actually hear the silence. When she stepped away from the judge I could hear snippets of various conversations and I felt as though everybody was looking at me, but I couldn't work out if I'd done something I shouldn't have.

I suppose I was mesmerised by her actions because I watched as she went to a large desk and picked up a whole stack of files and papers and she went around to the different people who wore the same types of robes and handed them some of the files and papers from her arms. When she returned to her chair, she sat down and again looked over at me and I turned away. I didn't want her looking at me; it made me feel very uncomfortable. That's when I saw the other woman. She was sitting at the far end of the large table and she had a strange-looking machine in front of her. It looked like an old-fashioned typewriter, but it looked too small to be one and I started to wonder what it might be.

When I looked back at the judge, he appeared to be reading something because he was looking down at his desk, his glasses perched on the tip of his nose; I thought they might fall off. Then he looked up at the man behind the glass and wood panelling then back down to whatever he was reading. I quickly glanced over to the man and could see his head was forward, as though he was praying or something—actually, I thought he'd fallen asleep and I wanted to go and give him a gentle shake, if only to let him know that he wasn't alone, but I can't remember why I'd thought that. Then something happened that I didn't see and I had to take my eyes away from him. I looked over to the judge, saw the woman in the black robe stand and turn to the man.

"The defendant will rise."

Her voice was quite shrill, like a squeaky bird, and it seemed to swirl around the room like a wind. I looked at the man behind the glass and watched him slowly stand. He looked so frightened, lost even, and I just wanted to go and stand next to him.

Everything seemed to happen so quickly after and I felt quite faint. The woman in the black robe was talking, but I didn't catch everything she said; my head was buzzing. I could see the other woman was busy tapping at the front of her little machine and other people dressed in those black robes shifting piles of paper and other stuff around the benches in front of them, not seeming to be bothered by what was being said. Then I realised that the first woman had stopped speaking and when I looked around the room, it felt as though everybody in there was looking at me. I wanted to leave … get up and walk out; I wanted to get away from all those pairs of eyes staring at me. I tried to look away, but I couldn't move; I was frozen to the chair. I began to panic, I could feel sweat running down my back and I looked over to the man behind the glass, thinking he would understand and show me somehow that I didn't have anything to worry about but, when I looked over, he too was staring at me. I could see he had tears in his eyes and all I wanted to do was go to him and hug him; I wanted him to know he had a friend.

Words started to fill my head and I knew they were not mine, they were not my thoughts and I was definitely not speaking. The word 'Guilty' snapped me out of whatever trance I was in and it sounded so … final and it was said with such force, vehement in the extreme. I felt my own tears well up and I reached for the tissues I knew I had in my pocket. I felt my anger building up and I wanted to shout at the judge and tell him he was so wrong. Through the haze of my tears, I looked over to where he was sitting at his bench with his expensive suit and dull-coloured tie and saw that he was looking straight back at me. I wanted to get up out of my chair and go and give this pompous-looking man a piece of my mind until I saw that he had a sheet of paper in his hand that looked vaguely familiar. It looked pink in colour and I remembered from somewhere in the back of my mind that I had writing paper that was the same. I wiped my eyes and took some deep breaths to calm myself, although my heart was still beating nineteen to the dozen. I watched as he read the letter, briefly look over to me and then to the lonely man sitting behind the glass.

*

When the judge spoke, his voice reflected a total difference to what I'd thought his character was; it held a deep compassion that radiated around the room like a warm blanket.

"I find you guilty of the charge and it is my duty to pass sentence. However, before I carry out that duty, I have been asked to read a statement to the court. I have read the statement many times and I must say that I agree fully with what it says and what it implies with regard to this case." He paused and looked at me and I swear he gave a warm smile.

He continued, *"The pain and suffering you caused in that moment of absolute recklessness will no doubt haunt you for the rest of your life. It can never go away and you have to rebuild a life around those memories. However, you were fully aware of the potential consequences when you got into your car after celebrating your wedding anniversary and you chose to drive in a manner that did, in fact, prove to be horrendous in its outcome. I have no doubt it is one anniversary you will never forget.*

I have in my hand a letter from the injured party. It states as a matter of fact that, no matter what punishment I pass down to you, it can never compare to the punishment you already put yourself through on a daily basis. You have to live with the constant reminder of your actions and I agree with the letter's sentiment that you will never allow yourself to forget. I believe that you too are a victim; however, I urge you to make whatever arrangements are necessary for the help you so obviously need with your drinking. It is without doubt a sign of belief, trust and love that we see in court today; the other victim in this case has shown great courage to be here today to show the court that belief, trust and love for you sir."

He paused again and all the people in that courtroom turned their attention towards me and, after what felt like another lifetime, he continued:

"I therefore sentence you to four years' imprisonment, suspended and a driving ban of six months. I have greatly reassessed my initial thoughts of your sentence due to the facts given to me in this letter. You will need mobility for the ongoing treatment for your wife, but let me stress, should you breach any part of the sentence laid down by this court today, you will go to prison and you will serve the full term as I have stated. You are free to leave and the court wishes you both well in your uncertain future."

I looked over to the man behind the glass but he wasn't there and I began to panic again. I looked around frantically wanting, needing to find him. Then I saw him hugging a tall woman who was in a black robe and I knew he was crying.

When they turned to me, I said a silent thank you and she smiled and gave a little wave. I couldn't believe what had just happened and I know I was crying when my gorgeous man reached down and cupped my face in his hands and kissed my forehead; he was the man I'd fallen in love with more than twenty-seven years ago and I loved him as much in that moment as I did back then.

"Come on sweetheart, let's get out of here and go and celebrate with a nice coffee, what do you say?" I looked up into his beautiful blue eyes and made some kind of noise because he released the brake from my wheelchair and pushed me towards the courtroom door.

*

I know I could've lost him on that day and I thank the judge every day for allowing my gorgeous man to come home and look after me. It's not been easy for either of us but we get by and we've had our fair share of struggles, but we also have a great laugh too. I'm getting stronger as each day passes and they say I might even be able to walk again—someday. I'm also beginning to start making sense when I try to speak, but it doesn't matter really; I have the man I love in my life and, although he gets things wrong every now and then, he's brilliant, patient and … gorgeous, so all things considered, we're doing pretty well.

----- ~ -----

Eternal

Sunday 22nd February 2004
Tobias and Monica Collingwood could never be labelled as a typical married couple. From the outside, they seemed to be living their lives as life was supposed to be lived rather than how society dictated. There was never anything they couldn't or wouldn't do for anyone. Their relationship was the envy of a few, but inspirational for many more. They would often be seen wandering around the local market town hand in hand, laughing heartily or giggling like teenage school kids. Whenever asked about their apparent happiness and love for each other, they both answered in the same way; they had met each other very early in their lives and that their love had grown stronger as each day passed. They had witnessed many times couples who had suffered in marriage where love had died, either through natural causes and passed on to somewhere where dreams became reality, or had died in the divorce courts. Monica was especially good with helping those bereaved with grief and also helping those lives that had been shattered into tiny pieces because of lost respect and trust. Toby was always amazed by Monica and her adept ways of helping, but had learned to expect it over the years. Theirs was the perfect relationship with no secrets—except one by Monica; she had kept it from her husband, lover and friend for the whole of their lives together, but she knew it was approaching the time to tell him.

*

Toby was concerned by what he'd seen in Monica over the past few days. She didn't seem to be her usual happy self. He first noticed something was different the previous weekend when they were making love; she seemed to be distant towards him. It was just as emphasised when they showered together that morning and for the first time in his life he didn't know how to talk to her about it. He felt uncomfortable when he thought about it, which in turn made him irritable towards her. He tried to dismiss it from his mind, but knew in his heart that something wasn't right.

Rays of sunlight crept into the conservatory through the blinds and he could feel the warmth on his shoulders. He tossed the Sunday paper onto the empty chair next to him, the chair that would usually be occupied by Monica, but for some reason she was still in the kitchen; he called to her but she didn't reply. He gazed out onto the garden, his mind racing from one absurd scenario to another and he felt strange thinking the unthinkable. Just as he was about to go and find out why she was obviously avoiding him she appeared at the doorway; she was holding two cups of black coffee and her hands were shaking. He froze when he saw that she had been crying, all of his unthinkable thoughts filling his imagination. He stood slowly. "What's wrong, Moni? You've been crying." He took the cups from her and put them on the table, then almost forced her to sit in her vacant chair, kneeling beside her. As she wiped her eyes with the back of her hand and tried to give an excuse about chopping onions, her tear-filled splutter stopped her mid-sentence and he pulled her close; his Moni was suffering and he didn't like it.

After a short while, Monica had gathered herself and asked Toby to sit in the chair opposite her. "We need to talk, my love," she said, her voice almost breaking again.

Toby was utterly mystified but did as she asked, noticing that she never once took her eyes from his. "What is it? What's wrong?" he asked, his heart pounding, the unthinkable thoughts emerging ever-strong in his imagination. Monica sniffed loudly and wiped the last tears with her palm, straightened herself in the chair and reached over and took Toby's hand in hers. "For all of my life, I have known you to have loved me unconditionally; you have given to me the very essence of your being and I hope I have shown you the same in return. We have lived and loved every day of our lives, safe in that knowledge that there was nothing on this earth that could've torn it away from either one of us and I have been happiest when I've been with you." Her voice was soft but determined. Toby sat, motionless, listening to words that felt like clouds covering his ears. He knew she was talking, but as each word came forth, it seemed to be coming from a faraway place. "Today is a day I've known about all along, right from our very first meeting …" she continued, her eyes fixed on his, "… a day that I've dreaded with all my heart, but also a day I've wanted to share with you forever. You can feel it already, my sweet; you know there is something happening and all I am able to do is be here to help you."

Toby leaned back in the chair and thought he saw Monica's hands glowing. He began to feel dizzy and blinked to clear the mist that seemed to be forming in his eyes. "Close your eyes, my darling," came as a whisper and he slowly slipped into what he thought was a deep sleep. "Hold my hand, Toby, and I'll share everything with you, you will know love as it has never been expressed in this world." He drifted along on clouds that felt like how he felt—comfortable, warm and safe. He searched for Monica and she appeared in front of him.

"Moni, where … what's happening, Moni … where are we …?" His voice sounded strange to him, as though he was in a great theatre with every word echoing back to him.

"You're OK, my love, you are safe here, Toby," Monica said and then disappeared into the breeze. Toby closed his eyes and wept.

*

He woke with a start; the dream had felt so real that the sweat on his forehead began to trickle down his face. He nervously looked around the conservatory, wanting to find everything was as he'd remembered. He leaned forward in the chair and put his face in his hands, he'd never experienced anything like that before and he felt scared. He called for Monica and when she didn't reply he tried to stand and go look for her, but he couldn't raise himself up. It was as though the chair was not letting him go. He started to panic when he tried to lift himself up again. More sweat began to form, only this time it seemed to be all over his face and in his hands. He looked over to the doorway, and with his head spinning he called for Monica; his voice sounded weak to him and he cried out again. He started to feel hot and strange inside; he couldn't think straight, he yelled out at the top of his voice. As he slipped away, he caught a glimpse of his beloved wife kneeling at his side. Her smile seemed to calm him and he tried to smile back for her, but he somehow knew he'd failed. He heard her whispering to him just as she did earlier, in his dream, "You are OK my love, you are safe here, I'm here to take care of you my darling." He tried to answer, but the words wouldn't come. He gazed into her soft hazel eyes and drifted again into a deep sleep.

He woke slowly to the sound of his name being repeated and tried to focus on the face above him. He lifted his arm and gently stroked the cheek of his wife and smiled. "I've had the most amazing dream, sweetheart; it was so beautiful, so ..." He felt her touch and something strange; as though she was filling his entire body with new emotions; feelings he'd never experienced before. "I feel so tired all of a sudden," he said and closed his eyes, but soon opened them again when he felt a burning sensation at the back of his ears and at the base of his neck. Fear filled his heart, even when he could see Monica holding his head between her hands. "What ... what are you doing ... what are you doing to me, Moni?" Panic rose in his chest and he tried to push her away, but his arms would not move.

Monica smiled and 'shushed' him constantly, her grip gentle on his head. "It's OK, Toby, I need to do this for you." She moved around to his side, never taking her hands from his head. He was sweating and he could feel the burn filling his head and he tried to speak, but no words would form; his eyes searched for Monica, his hands gripped the arm of the chair. He was locked in and nothing he thought about doing happened.

"I know you are scared, Toby, but you must let me finish." Monica's voice filled his head and he tried to turn to see her. She stepped into view and he could see there were tears in her eyes. His own eyes questioned her and she smiled. "It *is* OK, Toby. I know you are scared, but what is happening is something beautiful— it won't be long, I promise you, and when it is complete you will understand." He felt her voice fill his head in a whisper that penetrated through to his soul, but he never saw her lips move. He felt calming warmth begin to flow through his veins and his body relax in the soft chair.

He heard soft voices singing and what he thought was a breeze on his face, and when he tried to open his eyes, they were locked shut but he didn't panic; he relaxed more and felt lifted from the chair; he was giddy with the emotions floating through him as though he was drifting along on small rolling waves of the sea. All the while, he could make out the distinct voice of his Monica whispering to him.

"You are a special man, Toby; you were chosen on the day of your birth, as was I, when I was born. We are here to help others in their worlds. We transcend time and all of the universe's limitations; we have been chosen by The Highest Power to live, learn and to share our love with many. We are here to show how love will always hold worlds together—every world will survive. It was written in the long ago—before life, created for this world, was decided; in the whispers of winds between those universes known and yet to be seen."

Toby's eyes rolled in his head and he saw beautiful spheres with turquoise stars; clouds of amber mists swirled by gold fingers of reds and blues. He could hear Monica's voice clearer now as she spoke of what had happened in the past and what he was to expect of his future.

"You were born of the light of Addendium in the year One Thousand Nine Hundred and Forty; of the second depiction and in the dawn of more of that depicted; so few are to be chosen—you have proved in your chosen belief; how you live and how to love within those realms. As a disciple to your chosen light you have earned eternal life. You are to live again; to again show the joy of life and love amongst your fellow beings. Your love—left for the others to speak of, to be remembered in their hearts—will endure the times of all the Universes of The Highest Power." Toby strained to hear more, but the soft voice of Monica faded to nothing. He bowed his head; a sense of loss filled his heart and a cold shiver ran over his skin.

When he woke, he felt like he'd slept like a newborn baby; he felt more alive than he'd ever felt before in his life. He wiped his eyes and saw Monica kneeling in front of him; her smile warmer than ever and her hand in his seemed to be giving him strength. "What has just happened to me—us?" he asked.

Monica kissed his hand then slowly stood; he saw that she was changed. She looked different, younger than he remembered; just as she did when he first met her.

"We have a lot to talk about sweetheart," she said and pulled him to his feet as though he was a small child. He pulled her close to him and kissed her full on the lips and she responded.

"I feel as though I'm fifty years younger," he said with a laugh, "… you look stunning … just as when we first met." He picked her up and twirled around, their laughter filling the room.

*

Sunday 29th February 2004

They spent the rest of the day making love with each other, stopping only to eat a small, very late lunch. Toby was impressed with his own stamina and staying power and he was as impressed with the energy and enthusiasm Monica showed. He remembered back to the days when they first met, and later how they had spent an entire weekend in bed at a seaside hotel on the Isle of Wight. He smiled when he remembered some of the looks they had received from other hotel guests. He closed his eyes to recapture that time.

"Yes, Toby, they were very good times."

Surprised, he opened his eyes and turned to Monica, "What … what are you talking about?" He spoke with that sense of loss coming back to him.

Monica turned onto her side and traced a finger over his chest. "That weekend on the Isle of Wight; February 1964, when we shocked most of the other hotel guests. It was your twenty-fourth birthday present from your parents and me …" she hesitated, allowing the information to sink into the mind of the man next to her. Her eyes sparkled when she recognised his remembering, "… we had just been married and we were on our honeymoon, but what you didn't know—but must accept and understand—is that I am older than you believe me to be…" She watched as he replayed the memory and assimilated it into his acceptance and understanding. Toby raised himself up onto his elbow and looked down at her, questions cascading through his consciousness of this particular time and of a time far into her past.

"Yes, Toby …" she spoke softly, "… I am a lot older than you are; in fact I am exactly one hundred years older. I was born on the 29th February, in the year 1840. Today, 29th February 2004, I am celebrating my birthday just as you are but—I am 164 years old."

She smiled. Toby stared for a moment then slumped down into his pillow. "What does this all mean?" he asked with a sigh.

Monica leaned over onto him and kissed his cheek. "We are unique in our being; we were chosen because we were born of the second depiction—February; and, in the dawn of more of that depicted—the twenty-ninth. We have been chosen to carry on our love of life and of life itself, to the others of the future. We have been blessed with eternal life so that we can share life and love with those born of the same as we were. When we connect, we show the people of this earth how to live happily and how to love without condition." She paused. "Only … there are two things we are not able to do; the first is that we are unable to have children and the second is that once Addendium has shown itself to the chosen, we have to separate and take on another life in another time." She leaned forward and rested her cheek on his chest.

Toby stroked her hair. "And what of this life? What happens to us now?"

Monica took a deep breath. "At the first stroke of midnight, we will cease to exist as life for Tobias and Monica Collingwood; they will expire and we will move to another birth of the twenty-ninth of February. We will not remember anything of this life, but we will take all of our love to share with those which our new life touches."

Toby kissed her hair, hugging her close when he heard the first strike of midnight, his heart full of love for Monica and The Highest Power.

----- ~ -----

Secrets

"Morning James, how are you feeling today? Better, I hope. Now, we've to change your dressings and your bedding, but I'll go and get Mary and we'll give you a bed bath first."

'That's Nurse Jackie Stamp; she's a brilliant nurse and quite chatty really … but that's OK. You see, I had a bit of an accident and she takes real good care of me. Obviously, she's not the only one who looks after me, that would be silly to suggest; but she is one of those nurses you hear about or see on television in dramas. She reminds me a bit of my old Aunt Matilda; she was a nurse too and a very strict one at that. Nurse Jackie is just like her, old-fashioned but full of love and caring. She's the kind of nurse who will do that little bit more for her patients, especially if she believes it's for the best; she doesn't like to see *her* patients suffer. She's said that to me many times. She's a very thoughtful person, too. You know, she always covers me over whenever they give me a bed bath; she says it's to help me maintain my dignity. I wish all the nurses in here were like Jackie Stamp.

'When Jackie and Mary get together there is always lots of laughter. They treat me as if I was gold and I don't mean they treat me as if I'm just a heavy lump of metal. They treat me like I'm a delicate sliver of that precious metal; if they're too rough, I could bend and break. There is a lot of banter and chat and stuff when Jackie and Mary are working together, even gossip, but they make me promise never to tell a soul. Believe me,

I could tell you things that would make your eyes water and I could also tell you a couple of things that would break your heart, but I won't.

'The other day I heard Mary complaining how the new timetable has reduced her weekly and monthly hours and that it might also mean that she doesn't get to work with Jackie as often. I know Jackie was upset too because she talked to me about it after the letters were sent out last month. It seems that in cutting costs—or should I say, 'making more effective use of the workforce'—nurses like Jackie and Mary will probably lose ten hours from their shifts. Now I know there are a lot of people who wouldn't mind working less hours but I forgot to say, Jackie is a single mum and needs all the hours she can get, so that she can keep her daughter in the pre-school placement and also so that she can keep working because she doesn't want to stop and start claiming benefits. She gets really upset when she talks about it. In fact, she actually told me that she'd already applied for a position as a theatre nurse but wasn't sure if she really wanted it. It would mean she would have to work a full week of nights every second week of the month and that would mean she wouldn't see her daughter. I haven't told her that Mary applied for the job too … a promise of confidentiality. Personally, I think that of the two, Mary is more likely to take the job because she's older than Jackie and her kids have grown up and left home.

'Jackie was saying yesterday, I think, that she has the task of training another two new HCAs. She said that she was disappointed with the people who wanted to be Health Care Assistants, because they seemed to lack the very basic need of compassion for the vocation of becoming a care worker. She said that all they wanted to do was come in to work then just stand around tapping out messages on their mobile phones. They weren't interested in what the work actually entailed and that she had witnessed one or two incidents where the patients were treated like animals waiting to be sent to the morgue. She blamed it all on the lack of a good solid education from schools but more importantly, a good education from their parents.

'When Jackie starts on about the ways the youngsters of today have no respect for their elders and each other, she gets really animated. I think she had a strict upbringing … either that, or she really is an angel sent to show everyone how things should be done. She said her first new trainee would be in late tomorrow morning … apparently this new girl has an appointment with the dentist or something, which means she can't start the shift at seven thirty like everyone else. I don't think Jackie believes that though. I think she thinks it's because the girl can't get up in the mornings. We'll see, I suppose, but I'm a bit worried myself that this new girl might start treating me like someone waiting to be moved to the morgue, although I'm not that old, only thirty, and expecting to live to a ripe old age. I haven't said anything to Jackie about my concerns though … yet, she has enough to worry about.

'Another nurse popped in earlier, Jenny, from A & E; she's another good friend of Jackie's and they were making plans to go out at the weekend. It seems that Jenny is in the final stages of a divorce and wants to get back out in the singles scene and because Jackie is attractive and young, Jenny said that she would be the perfect person to go out with because she would attract all the good-looking men. Now, I can't give an opinion about whether Jenny is good or bad looking, but what I can do is pass on that her 'soon-to-be' ex-husband was nasty and treated her badly. I didn't see the bruise on the top of her thigh when she showed it to Jackie a few weeks ago, but I do remember them both telling me not to look because it was quite high up on her inner thigh … I wouldn't have minded having a look though.

'I hope you're not bored with me telling you all this stuff, it can get quite boring here. Like I said earlier, I had a bit of an accident and I'm reliant on Jackie and Mary … Jackie, mostly, because she's what is called my 'primary carer' and I have to say she is doing an absolutely brilliant job. I can't say that I can easily interact with everybody here but there is a definite connection between me and Jackie as she seems to know all the little things I need and when I need them. It's funny, because I get the feeling I've known Jackie all my life and we share so much together.'

"Good morning, Doctor Meredith, there are no discernible or significant changes in James today. Can I ask doctor; do you think he will ever come out of this coma?"

----- ~ -----

A Father's Pain

It felt strange to be back in the maternity hospital again ... after such a long time. When I walked into the corridor leading to the delivery suites, a cold shiver ran down my spine ... memories began to flood my head. They brought back the same feelings I had when I was about to become a father for the first time. I can't say if I was scared or excited—or both. What I do remember about that time are the mixed feelings as they surfaced again; how painful the whole experience was—very painful. I've learned over the years how different it is being a father and a dad. I suppose the only way I can describe those differences is by saying that you have to be a father to a daughter and a dad to a boy ... my firstborn was my son.

*

Back then, for me, everything during the first few weeks and months was a doddle really. I didn't suffer the morning sickness, which seemed to be there morning, noon and night, nor did I suffer any of the other million-and-one ailments women go through when they are pregnant and I'm not making light of it either—I wouldn't dare. What I mean is that I was working, so I missed all of that early stuff. Samantha was working too—she insisted— and there was nothing I could do that would've changed her mind. She was a very determined young woman; she had a mind of her own and it was one of the many things that attracted me to her and I so easily fell in love with her. It's a love I still have after all these years.

We didn't go out much after about month five because we were saving for when baby came. I would come home from work, help with the evening meal then, when everything was cleaned and tidied away, we would stretch out on the bed and listen to music or watch the small television that was perched in the corner of our one-bedroomed flat. We would talk for hours about our future and stuff, as normal twenty-somethings would, and inevitably, we'd end up talking about baby stuff—like which names of parents we'd use or not use. I can't say we ever argued, but I do remember it was fun and scary all at the same time. As time went on and 'bump' got bigger and more restless, I remember having a few heated words with Sam about her working long hours and I also remember getting quite an ear-bashing, so I left the subject alone for a few days. On the whole, we were content and happy—very happy.

*

I'll remember that Sunday for as long as I live. Sam and I had breakfasted, showered and she'd started to feel uncomfortable, an ache in her side, so I got her to lie down, hoping that the ache would go away—it didn't. She was still feeling bad at around three in the afternoon and—like the good, soon-to-be-dad I was—I called my mother. I told her what had been going on and she suggested that we get to the hospital so that Sam could be checked over. The baby wasn't due for another three weeks and it never occurred to either of us that she could actually be having her first contractions. My immediate concern, after I'd called Mum, was how I was going to get Sam to the hospital because I didn't drive back then, so I called my mum again. My younger sister told me that mum and dad were already on their way to pick us up and take us.

Now, I have to say at this point, my father and Sam didn't get along; they had this 'love-hate' relationship—they loved to hate each other. The reality was that he simply didn't know how to be around strong women. He couldn't cope with the fact that life had moved on and women were now liberated and being treated equal—but more importantly—with respect. He was still of the mind that women were supposed to be at home looking after the house for when the *'master'* came home from a hard day's work. Her job, as he saw it, was that she was supposed to have his dinner ready and on the table—and to look after the kids. He was extremely old-fashioned and I say this myself, his kind should've been burned at the stake—and yes, you guessed, we didn't get along too well either. Anyway, we got ourselves ready. I carried the hospital overnight bag and it still makes me smile when I look back and see Sam striding out of the front door to my father's car, sliding into the back seat as though nothing was wrong—as though it was just another ordinary Sunday afternoon. She didn't take shit from anybody and I loved her for it.

2

When we arrived at the hospital, we were taken to a side ward, a small room down a very long corridor and just after a set of yellow fire doors. Sam was helped onto the bed and then an over-enthusiastic young nurse started fussing around her; something that Sam found very annoying—and I know when she gets annoyed. I was ushered to the back of the room and told to sit in the chair next to a very large window and, believe me, I did as I was told; that nurse may have been enthusiastic, but she was also mean-looking.

During those initial minutes, I felt like the third person on a first date. Admittedly, I didn't have a clue as to what was going on and I honestly thought they were just going to give Sam a quick examination, tell us everything was OK, give her some kind of pain relief then send us home again. The thought that I could become a father that night never once entered my head—not even after we'd been in that room for more than two hours. I did have a go with the gas and air and Sam was calm and chatty—so I was calm and chatty—at least whenever anybody gave me a second thought. Whilst they were doing whatever it was they were doing to Sam in those first few minutes, I looked out of the window and saw a tall, lighted church spire across the road. Its silver coloured tip reminded me of a long finger pointing towards the sky and, for some unexplained reason, I said a silent prayer.

Things got hectic around half ten that evening. I could see Sam was in pain—a lot of pain—and no matter what pain relief they gave her, it didn't appear to work. The gas and air was a total waste of time and I lost count of the number of times I wiped away her tears. They eventually made me wear a gown that made me look like some clown from the circus and I tried to help take her mind off the pain by playing the fool, obviously when nobody else was around, but it didn't always work and I knew she was hiding the severity of her pain from me. And, I'm ashamed to say that that was when I didn't like her very much. We had agreed that since I was a big part of making the baby, we were going to share all the moments of the birth and, although I couldn't feel her pain, I wanted to be a full partner of it all and, selfishly, I felt left out at times. I know it was selfish, but it was our agreement; we were going to share every bit of the delivery as well as our lives afterwards. There was a time when I felt closest when she was holding my hand; and she was almost screaming at me that we were 'never' doing it again—and I thought she meant … well, she later told me that she meant we weren't having another baby—ever … and I believed her. My knuckles haven't been the same since, in fact, and I still have one that doesn't line up with the others. With her pain I felt so useless, but I can guarantee, if I could've taken her pain, I would've—in a heartbeat. I hated seeing her like that.

*

At six minutes after midnight, I became a father—I was a dad for the first time. I was so proud and excited and every other emotion you can think of. I wanted to go out into the streets and shout it at the top of my voice— I was a dad. I watched open-mouthed when they put our little boy on Sam's stomach, then handed me a pair of long-handled scissors so I could cut the cord; I know

I was crying when I did. I'd already done a very quick count of arms and legs and one of the nurses said that I had actually brought him into the world by cutting the cord. I was lost to the world around me and it took a few moments to notice that a couple more nurses had come into the room who then took my boy away. I don't know why, but I sensed something wasn't right. He'd looked OK to me, two arms and legs, a nice pair of ears, a full head of hair and a healthy set of lungs.

There was a lot of attention around Sam, and I have to say there is a certain moral indignity to a situation where you are watching a bunch of strangers prodding and poking around the intimate parts of the mother of your child, whose legs are up in the air. You just know that she is very distressed and there's nothing you can do. To say I was uncomfortable would be an understatement, and when I asked what was going on, I was told not to worry, 'just a few minor complications' that needed to be sorted.

I heard our boy's cries and turned to watch the nurse recording his details. She was very fastidious in the way she counted his entire fingers and toes, etcetera. I was again struck in awe at the tiny bundle lying naked in a steel tray you'd normally associate with a grocer's shop for weighing spuds and stuff. His little arms were flailing about, his chunky legs were kicking invisible footballs and his cries could've been heard on the moon. When I looked back at Sam, I could see she was even more stressed and pale; I put it down to the time and effort she'd put in to having our child, and when I moved over to be by her side, I was unceremoniously shooed away like some unwanted cat.

The nurse who had been recording our boy's details tapped my arm and handed our son to me. I looked down and pulled the blanket away so I could see all of his face and I swear he opened his eyes and smiled. He was so small though—fragile, and it was then that I was hit by a fear I've never experienced before in my life. I cried—again—my tears dropping onto his blanket and something at the back of my mind said I had to be very careful about germs and infections and that all newborns were susceptible so I wiped my eyes with the back of my hand, drying it on the leg of my trousers. I moved away from the hubbub around Sam and took our new son to the window, talking to him all the time, as though he was already a grown man. I made promise after promise and lifted him so that he could see the church spire from the window and my fear returned; I turned to Sam for some kind of reassurance.

Sam was lying on her side watching us; she had a look in her eyes and I'm positive, even to this day, she knew exactly what was going through my head and smiled, then held out her hand. I moved to her and with each careful step, I felt all my fears slip away. I knew we had nothing to fear—we were together and we had our son. I still choke up every time I think back to that particular moment … the night my life definitely changed.

At her bedside, 'new mum' wanted to hold her baby. She cried and smiled at the same time and I inched my backside onto the side of the bed, despite the scowls I was getting from the biggest nurse in the room. As far as I was concerned, we were family and nothing and nobody was ever going to get in between us. I slid my arm around Sam's shoulders, kissed her cheek, and whispered, 'Thank you,' because I couldn't think of anything else to say. She looked up at me and I could see she was still in pain but, being Sam, she smiled and said, 'I love you ... and our son, of course.' Her voice was croaky and I asked for a glass of water for her and helped her take a few sips. I know this is a cliché but, at that moment, my life was complete; I had Sam, my son and everything was brilliant. For me, she was the world's most beautiful person—mother and I fell in love all over again.

3

It was awkward sitting on the side of the bed with Sam still being fussed over with her trying to feed baby. I'd caught bits of hushed conversations and I knew I'd be asked to leave, but I was going to stay as long as I could. Although in reality it was probably longer, it felt no time had passed since I thought I'd be ushered away when I was asked to go and wait in the waiting area. I kissed Sam and told her that I'd be back before she went to the ward and that I would call Mum and Dad with our news. When I got to the waiting area, one of the nurses had followed me and explained the minor complications were with the detachment of the placenta; it wasn't detaching as it should. We talked a while and I decided to stay so I could say goodnight to Sam properly. In that waiting area, I went through a million and one emotions, thoughts and fears.

*

The next thing I remember about that night was that it was about half past three in the morning. I was sitting on a cold, damp bench in the car park waiting for my parents to pick me up. I was staring through a tear-filled haze at the church spire across the road, with its silver-coloured finger pointing towards whatever heaven there was … my heart shattered into a billion pieces—Sam had died at one-thirty-seven. It seemed the minor complications were not so minor after all. I screamed at the church with its spire wanting to know why … why He had allowed my love—my life—to die. He knew I had been left alone and that I was a brand new father—a dad. When my parents arrived, all they found was a broken man.

*

"Are you OK, Dad?" The sound of my son's voice woke me from my memories ... or should I say nightmares. I looked up into the eyes of a man who had become my world. Whenever I looked at him, he always reminded me of certain traits of his mother. He had her character and charm—and her eyes. I saw the same anxiety—a fear in his eyes, just like Sam had, when she was lying on her side in the bed when I had our boy in my arms by the window all those years ago. He looked older than his twenty-three years, but he was as handsome as she was beautiful.

I gazed up and down the corridor recognising the yellow fire doors, the room to the side, and I choked back tears as those memories tried to fill my head again. I coughed to clear my throat and stood.

"I'm fine, son ... I'm fine, just a few old memories, that's all." He reached over and squeezed my shoulder and nodded; I smiled as best I could, humbled by his silent understanding. I stepped over to the window quickly brushing away my tears. I could see that very little had changed of the view from there. This was the first time I'd set foot in the place since picking up my boy after what had happened ... but today, I was here to give whatever support I could to my son who was about to become a father—or a dad—for the first time. From where I was standing, I could just about see the tip of the church spire with its silver finger pointing upwards, and I said a silent prayer. I prayed that our son—mine and Sam's—would never know the pain I suffered all those years ago.

----- ~ -----

Home for Christmas

At the outbreak of World War I, many young men enlisted into the army and other services before they had reached the age of consent. Many of those brave men never returned home to their families.

As the author of this story, I do not have first-hand knowledge of any such situations.

The story is fiction; however, I would like to dedicate it to the memory of those young soldiers who never came back and to those who still fight today to keep our world secure and free of tyranny.

~~~~~~~~~~~~~~~~~~~

Mum,
I know you will be most upset when you read this, but I want you to know that I will love you and Dad for all time. Please try not to be too angry with me because this is something I must do. It is not a decision I made easily; in fact, I still have doubts about what I am about to embark on. I know in my heart I want to go and fight for our King and country, although I have wondered if I should wait a while.

I know we all expected the news about our going to war with Germany. However, I don't think any of us expected it to happen so quickly.

When I spoke with the Captain at the recruiting office, he said, unofficially of course, that it was not expected to last too long and that I should be home for Christmas.

Please tell little Andrew he can sleep in my bed, but only until I come home and that I will be thinking of him.

Tell Dad I promise to keep my head down and I'll be thinking of you all every day.

> *Your loving son,*
> *Henry-George.*
> *Tuesday 4th August 1914*

Wednesday 5th August 1914

Mary-Louise Hyland was sitting at the kitchen table, reading the letter again; she'd already lost count of the number of times she'd read it, but felt it was her only link to her son now that he had gone. She folded the single sheet and placed it gently onto the table. She stared at it for a while; her tears had dried, but she knew more of them weren't too far away. Absentmindedly, she rolled the tea towel in her hands over and over not really knowing what to do. She wanted to send Andrew to fetch his father and get him to go and bring her son back, but they didn't know exactly where he was. They knew of the recruiting office in the town, but they had been little help. She remembered back to when they first opened the letter, how they had run, almost, to the office and demand their son be sent home; then, how the sergeant at the desk had said the boys had already left for the training camp. She leaned back in her chair as images filled her thoughts; she could see young Henry-George in his christening gown; then, as a small boy playing in the yard with his toys. She screamed at the letter, "You are seventeen, Henry-George … you are only seventeen …" Her tears ran down her cheeks and she buried her face in the towel, her sobs muffled.

Thursday 12th November 1914

They had heard nothing from Henry-George with the exception of the two letters he'd sent whilst at the training camp. The first told them of how excited he was at the camp and how his training was hard and sometimes difficult. He also said that he'd started shaving and that he had finally been issued with his very own rifle and bayonet. The second letter was more disturbing. It explained how he would be part of the reinforcements of the expeditionary force that had been sent to France earlier in the year. He said he couldn't go into detail because the squadron corporal monitored all outgoing mail. A third letter had arrived a few days ago without any indication from where it had been sent or on what date. In it, he said they'd all arrived safely and that some of the lads had been seasick all the way over, but he had managed to keep everything down—due to his 'strong constitution' was the words he'd used.

Mary-Louise was standing at the sink staring out of the window, her mind wandering from one disturbing image to another. She and her husband had read the news in the paper of some of the injuries 'their' boys had received during the first encounter with the enemy. A cold chill ran down her spine at the thought of her son, Henry-George, being injured in such a way. She knew she would never stop fretting about him and had been to see the doctor to get something to help her sleep at nights. Thoughts of him lying in a ditch somewhere woke her most nights and she knew it was affecting her relationship with the rest of the family.

The sound of the front door closing snapped her from another daytime nightmare and she quickly finished washing the last pot and tried to smile when her husband walked into the room. She watched him drop his hat onto the table and slip off his coat. No words were exchanged, but he could tell by the redness around her eyes that she'd been crying. He stepped over to her and wrapped his arms around her, knowing it was hopeless trying to comfort the inconsolable. Although he tried to remain strong for her, it broke his heart to see her this way and he had accepted he was helpless in warding off her sense of loss. He felt her body shake as she sobbed and he fought back his own tears.

Tuesday 10th November 1914

Henry-George was half sitting against the sidewall of the trench with his rifle leaning on his thigh, his hands shaking as he tried to light the cigarette in the corner of his parched lips. The screams and moans of wounded comrades-in-arms filled the air and the smell of death mingled with clouds of cannon fire. He'd learned, early, that smoking was one way of disguising the awful stench and the only way to take away its taste. With the cigarette finally lit, he filled his lungs and blew a thin spiral of blue smoke down to his feet, remembering what his friend, Corporal 'Taffy' Davies, had told him when he'd first arrived at the front line.

"You don't want to let the enemy see you, see … they have eyes like hawks and if they see you, they shoot their bullets of death … you 'ave to blow your smoke down so's they can't see where you are … see."

He smiled at the thought of his oldest and wisest friend then instantly threw himself to the floor of the trench as clumps of earth showered down around him after the impact of another enemy shell exploded close by. "Shit." He yelled at nobody and everybody.

When the dust had settled, he crawled up to his knees and slapped away the dirt from his tunic with his cap then slipped it back onto his head. He pulled the cigarette from his mouth and blew on the end to see if it was still alight; it looked fairly dry, but soon came back to life. He picked up his rifle and leaned it against the battered and splintered timber of his ladder, wondering if it would still be strong enough to take his weight again.

When he'd finished his cigarette, he began readying himself for his next turn at firing at the enemy lines, which were less than two hundred yards away. His new corporal had devised a plan that he said 'would instil a fear in the hearts of every man over there' and 'create confusion amongst the senior ranks of the enemy' because they wouldn't know exactly how many troops were waiting this side. The plan was to lay down sporadic fire, at intermittent intervals, from different locations along the trench and thereby holding the enemy in their positions. Some of the corporal's words had confused Henry-George, but he followed orders without hesitation and since the man had been at the front for longer than any of his comrades. He had witnessed first-hand the devastating results of the new plan but, orders were orders, and he was not going to be the one to say anything.

With a final drag on the cigarette, he flicked it down into the ever-softening mud and adjusted his cap, sliding it backwards slightly, giving him a better sighting down the long muzzle of his rifle. He carefully checked the front and rear sights of the weapon, pinching out earth that had lodged in between the little prongs of metal when he had dived for cover. He checked and brushed dirt from the lever bolt and pulled it open and checked the chamber; everything looked clear and surprisingly clean, considering the number of times it had been in the mud. He checked the magazine was still in place and slowly turned to face the wall of the trench, glancing left and right before placing his mud-laden boot on the first rung of the flimsy-looking ladder. Sweat started to trickle down his back as he steadied himself before pushing up onto the next rung, his mind wandering to his little brother and his mother and he squeezed his eyes tight to clear his head to focus on the task at hand. He eased himself up and clung to the extended third rung with his free hand and hoped it, too, would take his weight. With bended knees, he swung a leg around the extended rung and lifted his rifle up to his side, purposely waving it left and right, knowing the long muzzle was now visible to all watching eyes. It was a ploy he had developed after seeing his friend Taffy get shot through the face four days ago; he shivered at the memory. He choked back the bile in his throat and glanced over his shoulder, to where Taffy's cap still lay in the trench. He hadn't had the strength, let alone the will, to move it and could see the dark stain of dried blood around the hole at the back. His breathing was heavy and he turned away, resting his head against the wood of the ladder, his eyes tightly shut, his fear growing inside. The muscles in his legs were burning, but he didn't care, he wanted to be away from there ... away from the noise and screams of dying men. He wanted to be a hundred miles from the smell and the mud—he wanted to be at home with his mother and father and his annoying little brother. He fought back his tears and screamed, but it went unheard as the ear-shattering blast of artillery fire erupted behind him. He hunched further down on the ladder, praying that each shell found its mark, killing the entire enemy army, putting an end to a war he should never have volunteered to join.

When the barrage had finished he slid his rifle up his side and pulled back on the bolt to chamber his first round. He lifted it further, slipping the butt into his shoulder and easing his chin against the stock, nodding slowly and methodically to get his focus on the muzzle's front and rear sights. It was an extremely awkward and uncomfortable position to be in, but he knew that by doing it, he'd survived longer than most and his accuracy of shot had been improved. He paused a moment longer, waiting for any kind of reaction from enemy lines. Then, in one swift movement, he straightened his legs, brought the muzzle to bear on the familiar parapet he'd fired at less than ten minutes ago and squeezed the trigger. The shot rang in his ears as he pulled the bolt back for a second shot, not ducking down behind the trench wall as he'd been taught. He caught a glimpse of movement to his left and quickly adjusted his aim and squeezed the trigger a second time. The deafening hollow click brought instant realisation that he'd not checked the magazine and he cursed himself. A distant crack sounded and almost immediately he felt his head jerk savagely sideways, lifting his entire body away from the wall and off the ladder. He dropped into the mud at the bottom of the trench like a stone, pain engulfing him like flames around a chunk of coal. Before consciousness left him, he saw his cap lying beside his old friend's, a small hole above the peak and to the side of the badge and a small dark stain already smudged into the fabric.

Tuesday 22nd December 1914

Mary-Louise had just finished putting the last of the decorations around the large mantel clock; a wedding gift her parents had given so many years ago. She was standing in front of the hearth in the parlour, admiring her handy work and, although her spirit was not in a festive mood, she knew she had to make an effort.

With the unused decorations packed into the old cardboard box, Mary-Louise took it upstairs. Whilst she was pushing the box under the bed, she heard the front door open and close and, not knowing the time, she assumed little Andrew had come home from playing out in the snow, wanting something hot to warm him. She called down, "I'll be down in a minute love; take a look in the parlour at the decorations … I think they look quite nice this year." A spark of excitement trickled through her and she sighed. "We'll make this a good Christmas …" she said to herself. When she stood, she almost instantly fainted down onto the bed when she saw her husband standing in the bedroom doorway; his face was ashen. He still had his work coat on and his hat in his hands, rolling it between his fingers by the rim. Mary-Louise slumped down onto the bed, horrific thoughts filled her head as her husband stepped over to her and sat down beside her, his eyes never leaving hers. She fell into his arms sobbing when he told her his news.

"There's news of Henry-George—he'll be home for Christmas."

----- ~ -----

Unanticipated

He could remember those meetings so vividly now. He had been at the head of one of the biggest shake-ups in more than three decades. It was his hands on the helm and it would be him steering reform forward.

The findings from the government's research indicated that one of two outcomes were the potential reactions. There could be outright acceptance or utter revolt. But he was confident that, after an initial 'minor' uprising, the new 'status quo' would prevail; he had publicly staked his Ministerial position on it.

History would remember the day; that of 1st February 2030, when his new Prison Reforms were implemented and practised from that day forward. The reforms were global; implementation initially was throughout the whole of the prison estates in England, Wales, Scotland, Northern Ireland and all Commonwealth Countries; phase two of his reforms would then go on to The United Europe Nations and finally, The World United Federation of Nations.

It had proved to be an extremely difficult struggle to persuade his fellow Ministers and Cabinet Members that what he was actually proposing was the best way forward. He remembered all the late nights, the days he'd missed his children's sports days, etc., arguments with his wife and other family members. He grimaced at the thought of the long hours of writing and rewriting pages of his proposals. The times he had presented it to the various committees, then having to revamp certain passages and paragraphs to appease particular committee members and member states. The time he'd spent in meetings and other important discussions; always pushing his ideas forward.

The most vivid of these memories were the countless meetings with the varying groups and associations who were expected to carry out the reforms. They had all been, at one point or another, during those initial meetings, opposed to such measures being employed within the prison estate. He remembered how he had held his ground on more than one occasion, how he had showed them who was the boss, so to speak. He had eventually persuaded each and every one of them that his way was the only way. At one point, he had to remind one of the groups that he had been personally selected by the United Prime Ministers, no less, to be the new Minister of Justice.

He couldn't remember the name of the chap from the Prison Officers' Association, but he clearly remembered how he had reacted to the proposal, how he'd embraced the rudimentary principles of the process and he saw how they could easily be implemented. The fact that he was a recent 'ex-military' man was an undeniable bonus. It was as if he could see the future, the long-term effect of the proposition and how it would have an immediate effect in the reduction of reoffending figures. Clearly, he was a man of vision, a man for future greatness within the profession, a future Governor. In fact, it was one of his observations that he, the Minister, had 'borrowed' and claimed to be his own. "There is 'no fear factor' within our prison systems today." It was all too repetitive; people were being sent to prison for crimes and receiving very lenient sentences. These people would do their 'time' and within weeks, in too many instances, re-offend, safe in the knowledge that prison wasn't all that difficult. Another of that chap's ideas was 'adopted' by the Minister's Office, in that a 'Good Dose of Discipline' was all that was needed. In fact, he remembered how both of those ideas had become slogans for the campaign. He remembered seeing the headline of the UK *Daily Mail*; **'A Dose of Discipline in our Prisons,' demands Minister**. The World *Sun* had run with; **'Bringing the "fear" back to prisoners'**. He settled back in his chair, reminiscing those memories and smiled.

He recalled the interview at the Beeb, how they'd tried to belittle him for bringing such brutal, draconian practices back into the prison system. He remembered how he'd explained that such measures were needed because the public were 'fed up' with footing the bill so that those men and women could live such easy lives. He agreed that for most offender's, prison was simply too easy, although it was 'no picnic', but, it was too soft on those who knew how to 'work' the system.

He sat forward in his chair and started to read through the reforms, taking in as much detail as he could. He recalled how he had worded each reform and how they would be implemented:

Mandatory for all prisoners:

Three Steps Back

i. When a person is convicted of a crime and the crime has a determinate prison term, all convicted persons will serve a minimum of **three (3) years**.

ii. All **Year One** convicted persons will serve in a facility designed to induce **discipline**. This induction programme will include courses designed to show how the criminal will learn **respect**.

iii. **Year One** convicted persons will be shown how to live in society, how to accept that they have wronged society and how they can work towards becoming better in themselves. They will be encouraged to think in ways of '**selflessness**' rather than '**selfishness**'.

iv. All convicted persons will maintain high levels of personal hygiene; keep cells clean and tidy. They will remain quiet at all times whilst in **Year One** facilities. Violations will result in additional time to the original sentence.

v. All convicted persons progressing to **Year Two** will have shown sufficient and unequivocal remorse for their crime. It is stressed, however, that commencement in a **Year Two** establishment for a convicted person can only be implemented once the convicted person has satisfactorily completed **Year One**. Transfer to a **Year Two** establishment, another specifically designed facility, can only be implemented at the discretion of the releasing authority of the **Year One** facility.

vi. All convicted persons entering a **Year Two** facility can expect a limited degree of autonomy throughout their daily life. They will be expected to display a discernible effort in self-reliance. All **Year Two** cells will have sufficient room for the potential installation and availability of white goods. All white goods will be purchased by the convicted person. The cells in all **Year Two** facilities will be of specific dimensions that will include private shower and toilet facilities.

vii. All **Year Two** cells will have '**Power Production Units**' installed for the use of the convicted person. These units will produce sufficient power to the cell when used by the convicted person. The convicted person will be expected to produce the power to use the facilities within the cell. Each item in the cell and/or purchased by the convicted person will have a calibrated unit displaying the required power to use the item and the amount of stored power (e.g. hot water for a fifteen-minute shower will require **One Hundred credits**). One credit is equal to three minutes' usage of the **PPU** (**Power Production Unit**). Any convicted person diagnosed by the medical team at the facility as being unfit, or incapable, of generating sufficient power to shower, will be allocated a credit level commensurate with the financial status of the convicted person prior to conviction.

viii. If a convicted person is deemed to have insufficient financial means, he/she will have the opportunity to sell power to the **Year Two** facility. The facility authority will agree sale and purchase prices with the convicted person individually; this agreement will be based on prescribed medical assessments of abilities. However, no facility authority will be allowed to purchase power credits at a rate that is less than the universal grid pricing system.

ix.   All convicted persons will be allocated visitation rights based on the severity of the crime committed. Listings of crimes and relevant visitation allocations will be issued, subject to formal request, to all convicted persons as part of the induction phase in **Year One** facilities. It is the responsibility of the convicted person to make formal representation for the lists through the authority of the facility. Failure to submit a formal request to the facility authority within the specified time will result in visitation rights being suspended for a minimum period of **Nine Months** after conviction date.

He sat back in his chair, pinching the bridge of his nose and squeezing his eyes shut, stifling his need to burst into tears once again. He slapped the back of his head in frustration, wanting to scream at the top of his voice, but his inner fear prevented him. He wanted everybody to know that this was all wrong; he was not supposed to be here, that he'd received numerous letters of support … from high-ranking officials and even state leaders. He'd had the support of his own wife and family and that of his own country's Prime Minister … to him, this was all WRONG.

He lashed out his arms wildly over the desk as his frustration burrowed deep into his psyche, knocking his tin cup off the desk and he watched it fall, clattering onto the bare concrete floor. He froze instantly; statue-like; he held his breath, praying that it had not been as loud as he thought it actually had been. The hiss of white-noise silence filled his ears; sweat forming on his entire body and straining to listen, he heard the distant footsteps approaching. He turned his head slowly, not wanting to make another sound and stared intently at the silver letterbox opening in the door. Minutes passed like hours and he began to shake, fear welling from deep inside, tears filling his eyes and cramps gripping his stomach. He wanted to vomit, bile filled his throat.

He watched in horror as the silver letterbox slid silently open and saw the face of Mr Turnkey. He could just see the top of the writing pad the officer held in his hands and then he heard the words he'd heard several times in the recent past, his early days of imprisonment, "Alpha X-ray 35559, Violation of order number IV, creating an unwarranted and unacceptable disturbance during reflection time in a Year One facility …" the officer paused momentarily, "Ninety days." The silver letterbox closed and he heard the footsteps gradually disappear from hearing and then focused on the sheet attached to the door above that silver strip of highly polished metal …

> **Convicted**: Historical: Sexual Assault, Sexual Harassment, Fraud
> **Sentence**: Four Years
> **Date of conviction**: 1st February 2038

He glanced at the digital wall calendar and watched as the extra days were painstakingly added. He did the calculation; he had now been in a **Year One** facility for more than four years. He slowly lowered himself into his chair and cried … silently.

----- ~ -----

Demons

Young Kenny Wilson was a bright boy who had loving parents and was close to all his various aunts, uncles and cousins. He was above average in school; in fact, he was doing very well. His last English and maths results put him in the top three of his class and some of his artwork was on permanent display in the school entrance hall.

He was a likeable lad who loved to play most sports and did quite well in them, too. He'd set a new house and school record for the hundred-metre sprint in the previous year's inter-house sports day and had been voted 'class prefect' for three years running. He had lots of friends and had recently joined the local scout troop that held their weekly 'scout night' on Thursdays. At age twelve, Kenny had little to worry about, or concern himself with; life was good and he enjoyed it to the full.

He had one 'best friend', Clive, and they did almost everything together. There was only ten months' difference in their ages, Kenny being the older of the two. They had adventures together during the long, hot summer holidays and sometimes at the weekends, when they were allowed to go night river fishing. They would catch the bus into Tewkesbury on the Friday evening and set up camp along the Severn or Avon, depending on their mood, and fish, enjoying their grown-up independence. They very rarely caught anything, but it was the time together they enjoyed.

It was during one of their night fishing weekends when their chat turned to the things that scared them.

Clive had admitted that he was more scared of growing up than anything else in the world. He said he'd recently heard his parents talking about money and never having enough and other things that made being a grown-up less desirable. Kenny had listened and hesitated before telling his best friend that his biggest fear, in the whole world, was the dark. Kenny Wilson had an acute fear of everything and anything that had to do with the night and darkness. When Clive pointed out that they were sitting on the bank of a river, on a Friday night, at nearly twenty-five past three in the morning, it made his confession a little bit more than unbelievable. It had taken until dawn for Kenny to convince his best friend why he had such a fear. He had explained that whenever he was with somebody else, his fear was almost non-existent and only got bad when he was alone; even at night in his own bedroom. Clive tried to hold back his laughter when he heard how his friend would use a torch to search under his bed before climbing in, to reassure himself that there was nothing or nobody there. He lost the battle and laughed loud and strong when he heard how Kenny would go rigid with fear whenever he heard strange and unfamiliar sounds in his house at night. They never spoke about the subject after that night.

*

Summer ended and they were still best friends. Kenny had celebrated his thirteenth birthday and Clive had joined the scouts, which they both attended regularly every Thursday evening. The big event of their year was when they learned that the building of the new scout hut had been completed and was now ready for the troop;

everybody was excited and eager to move. The change of scout night to a Friday evening was greeted with a little less enthusiasm by some members, but mostly by Kenny and Clive.

One Friday evening, when the nights were darker, Clive played a prank on Kenny that stretched their friendship to its limit. Their new route to and from the new scout hut took them along a path that had only one street lamp and Clive knew that the lamp was not working. On each side of the path were high hedges and gateways to houses, but it was the quickest way home. They had left the scout hut at the end of the meet and were walking home when Clive stopped to tie his shoelace. Kenny hadn't noticed and had carried on walking, but when he realised he was alone, he froze. He soon began to see demons and horrible slime-covered hands reaching out from the hedges and gateways; he was terrified. He slowly turned to look back, but Clive was nowhere to be seen. He called out for his best friend, but there was no reply. His heart was pounding and tears had filled his eyes. He didn't know what to do; he wanted to run, but his legs were solid pillars of stone. He turned back, too scared to move and didn't hear Clive sneak up behind him. There was no ghostly screeching or wolf-like howling; it was just a simple touch of the shoulder that set things off.

*

Clive watched from his bedroom window. He saw the ambulance arrive and he saw the wrapped body being wheeled out of the house down the street and loaded inside. He would never forget the look of absolute terror on the face of his best friend. He hadn't noticed the flashing blue lights, nor did he hear the siren when the ambulance drove away. However, he did see the three police officers walk up the path to his house and he did hear the knock on the front door and his mother call him down to speak with them.

*

Kenny had spent almost two months in hospital and in the last week, or so, had wondered why his best friend had not visited. When he arrived home, his visitors had been limited to family only. He was under strict observation and was not to be allowed to get overexcited. He was bored within days.

After lots of pleading and arguments with his parents and psychiatrist, he was eventually allowed to see his best friend. Their initial meeting was somewhat strained, but soon settled to their old, better days. It wasn't long before Clive became a daily visitor and both the psychiatrist and his parents were pleased with the improvements in Kenny's mental and physical health.

It was Kenny who brought the subject up first, not knowing the very strict instructions from doctors, psychiatrist and both sets of parents that Clive was never to mention or talk of the night in case Kenny had a 'turn'. He explained to Clive how the psychiatrist had showed him a technique where he could actually overcome his fear of the dark by tapping the fingers of one hand against his thumb and reciting a strong, reaffirming statement:

> 'Fear is: False Evidence Appearing Real
> and it's only in my head.'

They giggled when Kenny said he had tried to put a tune to it, but the words didn't help. They spent the morning trying to come up with a song that would fit, but failed.

Very soon, Kenny was pestering his parents, doctor and the psychiatrist about going back to scouts. He reassured them that he had conquered his fear and eventually convinced them. He was excited when his mother and father finally agreed to allow him to go the next Friday evening.

Although it was getting dark when he left his home to call at Clive's house to go to the meet, he was feeling very strong inside and they enjoyed the walk to the scout hut. They both laughed when Kenny reminded Clive of the night and even tried to play a similar trick on his friend.

It was early during the meet when Clive had an accident and was taken to hospital, and it took Kenny time to convince everybody there that he'd be OK on his own. When it was time to leave, he had already refused at least twenty offers of having somebody walk home with him and set off with determination and a sense of pride at his new-found strength. As he got closer to the pathway, he started reciting the statement about fear and walked, unhesitatingly, into the darkness.

Young Kenny Wilson never emerged from that dark pathway that Friday evening and was never seen again.

----- ~ -----

The Beautiful Game

I could not say … yet … if I was considered to be a full member of this exclusive clique, or if I ever would be, because these guys had been friends for a long time before I came along. There were three of them and they met almost every evening; they would play their game, chat and generally have fun. There was no particular leader of the trio, but there was definitely a level of respect for one another and, dare I say, a fondness between them. In the early weeks and months, I learned their lives were linked somehow, but it was something they never spoke of—a secret that none was prepared to divulge. I think this was one of the many reasons why I found myself attracted to their little group.

They were all very different in their characters and individual mannerisms, but there was also this underlying similarity about them; something that never really drew attention from outsiders, but if, or when, they allowed you close enough, it became more palpable—a commonality about their very existence. How I ever got the final invite to join the group would always be a mystery to me, but it was much appreciated—I had an inkling I would be part of the group for quite some time. The first few months was the hardest, if only in trying to understand their unique way of communication—their language was a hotchpotch of slang, mixed with Welsh and English—a kind of 'Welglish'—although I suspect two of them were Welsh by descent, but they never said. It took me at least four months to 'fine-tune' my listening to begin to understand them and even then, during those months, I felt that there was something being said that would be of interest and useful to me—but I couldn't understand a bloody word.

It would be unwise and unkind to name these individuals since they are quite sensitive about their 'lives' and how others perceive them. So, what I will do is give you my interpretation of how I see each character and hope that, should you recognise any of them, you would please keep it to yourself and accept there are laws that must be observed with regard to disclosing personal information about individuals. I'll do my best to give you an absolute, definitive description of each player of our game, but re-iterate, you cannot tell anybody about whom you might think you know I am talking about. I'm also doing this for my own sake, because I do not want to be held liable to any form of persecution from them if, or when, they read this.

I'm not going to put them in any particular order as players; again, because I don't want to suffer the consequences.

The first player can only be described as a cross between Charlie Chaplin and an emperor penguin. Apparently, he injured his back a while ago and this made him waddle from side to side when he walked. It became a habit which he never got out of. Though comical to watch, we all knew he suffered, plus we all know how a bad back can have such debilitating effects on our whole body and wellbeing. I'm sure you all know when you've suffered a 'twinge' and how it made you 'semi-stoop' whenever you had to go anywhere. Getting in and out of your car is a good example; every single muscle movement causes other pains in other parts of your body. This is how he suffered. He never encouraged sympathy, either, since he refused to do anything he'd been told, which was to rest. There were numerous times when all he did, all evening, was to whinge and whine about how bad his back actually was and to be honest, we just ignored him and carried on regardless. He was also a very bad loser. I remember quite recently that after just fifteen minutes or so he was behind and he started looking for excuses; he suddenly 'remembered' he had other things he should be doing. He was fidgety, up and down like the proverbial 'yo-yo', wanting to wander off and do those things—the more important things—rather than carry on with the game. It was quite off-putting at first, but we soon learned to ignore it all and carry on; having our own fun, playing our game with each other.

The second of the trio can only be likened to that of the old mother-in-law joke; the one about the Exocet missile … you know she's coming, but there's nothing you can do to stop her. He was just like that—but with a twist. Oh, you knew he was there and you eventually learned to know there was little, if anything, you could do to stop him. He said very little, but when he did he would have you either in fits of laughter, or in deep thought—thinking serious thoughts—about absolutely bloody nothing. There were no gems of any great importance or relevance to the here-and-now. However, all the while, he was building a score—a high score that inevitably became an unbeatable score—he was a right pain in the arse. He looks a lot older than he actually is and, when asked about it, he would simply say he'd lived a life of hard winters and long hot summers. I always saw him as most definitely the outdoors type, with his leathery, sun-kissed skin, grey hair and T-shirt tan. You know the one I mean; only the exposed parts of his body were tanned—the rest of him, his arms, body and legs were as white as snow, so that when he took his T-shirt off, which wasn't that often—he still looked as though he was wearing one—a T-shirt. However, THE most lethal weapon in his arsenal was when he broke wind. It could rip the hairs from your chest from the inside ... blow your socks off without removing your shoes—they could bring tears to your eyes to rival any onion, that's how bad they were. The real killers, though, were the 'silent' ones. You knew nothing of what was about to happen; it was only after you recognised the stupid smirk appear on his face that something 'was' coming—but by then, it was too late ... it was like a striking cobra—lightning fast and you were 'hit'. A strike so lethal that you were soon crawling around on the floor, clawing at your throat, gasping for clean, fresh air. Nightmare.

Now, the third in the trio didn't always take part in the game. This guy preferred to offer support, preferring to add his 'know-how' about how to go about playing the game. He would often give all of us advice on which way to play, etcetera; although, whenever he did grace us with his partaking of the evening game, he got it all spectacularly wrong. If there was ever a man born to get things wrong, this was he. I can only offer, as a physical description, to say he resembled (far too closely) the cartoon character from the film, *Casper the Friendly Ghost*. The tall, thin one with the large Dodo-like hook nose. Now, don't get me wrong, we all liked him because of the fact he was one hell of a good laugh to have around;

forever cracking silly jokes and making sarcastic comments when one of us screwed things up. He tended to stay in the background on a lot of occasions and I later found out it was because he was constantly worrying about other things. He worried about all the things 'he' had no control over, just as we all have at some point in our lives—but this guy had it down to a fine art. He never allowed himself the luxury of just 'being' in the moment. One of the annoying things about him was, whenever he got bored, or his head gave him time off from his worrying, he would try and bite the knee of Exocet. He would go after the guy's knee like a man possessed and, usually, just as he was about to take his turn. What made it more ridiculous was the fact that the man only had three teeth in his head. Picture, if you will, a man leaning over and trying to bite your knee. Imagine the sight of the man's head moving rapidly towards your knee and all you can see is the outline of three blackened teeth, in a wide open mouth, trying to bite you. It was as laughable as it was ridiculous, which obviously had an effect on the way Exocet played, and I have to say that at times it became annoying and off-putting, but again, it was just another of the things we learned to ignore.

Finally, I come to the hardest part of my story—probably. I've given you a basic description of the others and, I hope, I've achieved it. I'd like to think I've done it without causing too much distress and that I've not defamed anybody's character. I'm at the point where I have to tell you—about me.

So OK, I've been told I am opinionated and sarcastic, and a lot of other names which I can't put in here, but suffice to say, they are not complimentary. I've been likened to the character Victor Meldrew, which I have to say, probably fits me to a tee. I do complain, I do moan and I speak my mind. I also, apparently, use twenty words when three would be enough. I am the founding member of the unaffiliated club O.G.C. (Old Gits Club). There are two—no, three other members: my playing partners. We play our game and we do moan a lot … its part of the job, I suppose. Oh, and I don't like being cold which, given what I'm about to tell you, isn't something I have any control over. The game we play, every evening, come rain or shine, although there is very little in the way of sunshine since we play in the evenings … I say evenings, but in truth we play in the late evenings, when most people are either sleeping or just going to sleep. Well, anyway, the game we play is … golf. Now be honest, you weren't expecting that were you?

We play when all of you reading this are tucked up nicely in your warm, cosy beds, the stars are out, usually, the wind howls, sometimes—most times—as do the hounds, foxes and other creatures of the night. Owls can be a bit of a nuisance because they swoop at the most inappropriate times. We play our game when 'life' as you know it, is suspended, when you dream the dreams of a life to fulfil, of hopes and lives of success, family, friends … loved ones, present and those who have passed—passed on, that is. We *are* those friends and loved ones. We are the people who you miss and say your prayers for—and let me tell you, we hear those prayers and we thank you for not forgetting us. We play close to where we used to live, around your homes, your gardens and in the streets. So, if when you wake in the mornings and find that a favourite plant pot has been knocked over, or something isn't where you left it the night before, please don't fret about it. It's us, playing our little game in all the places where we know people, like yourselves, won't mind because you now know we are still around watching over you. We miss you as much as you do us, but we still keep in touch by our pot-knocking or 'stuff-moving'. We might be 'gone', but we surely are not dead and buried.

Oh ... and one last thing, to those of you who put 'remembrance' benches out as memorials. Please, think again about where you put them ... yes, we accept you've done it as a gesture of remembrance and it is more than likely you've chosen those particular spots because 'Old Uncle Harry would've liked it there', or, 'Mum loved to sit there in summer' ... but the truth is, it plays havoc with our game which is why we knock things over, or move things around. We don't do it on purpose ... we treat them as natural hazards; and to those with ponds—do you realise, losing a ball in an uncovered pond carries a two-stroke penalty! It's another shot penalty for every dead fish, too ... I'm down six shots on the leader board at the moment and all because my family love to have water in the gardens ... waterfalls, ornate ponds—everything—all of them—and I had a very big family!

So, in closing this little narrative; to all of you who claim to have seen something strange, or swear you've heard things going bump in the night ... and, for all those who say they don't believe in ghosts, you'd better start believing because—WE ARE HERE ... we are out here playing our special game of golf—and we are having the time of our lives—FORE!

----- ~ -----